BF
723
.T9
S74
1978

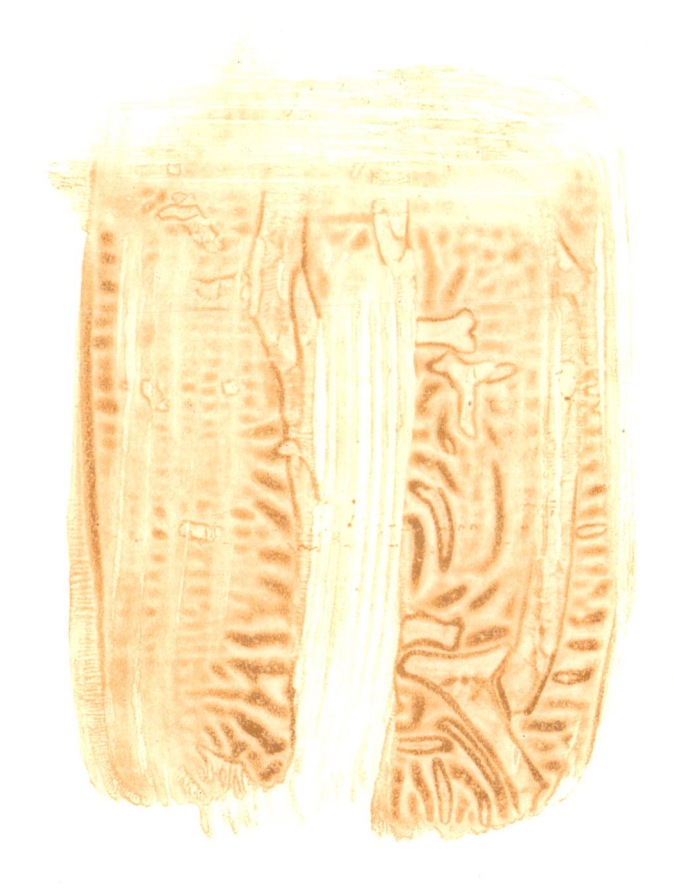

PARALLELS
A LOOK AT TWINS

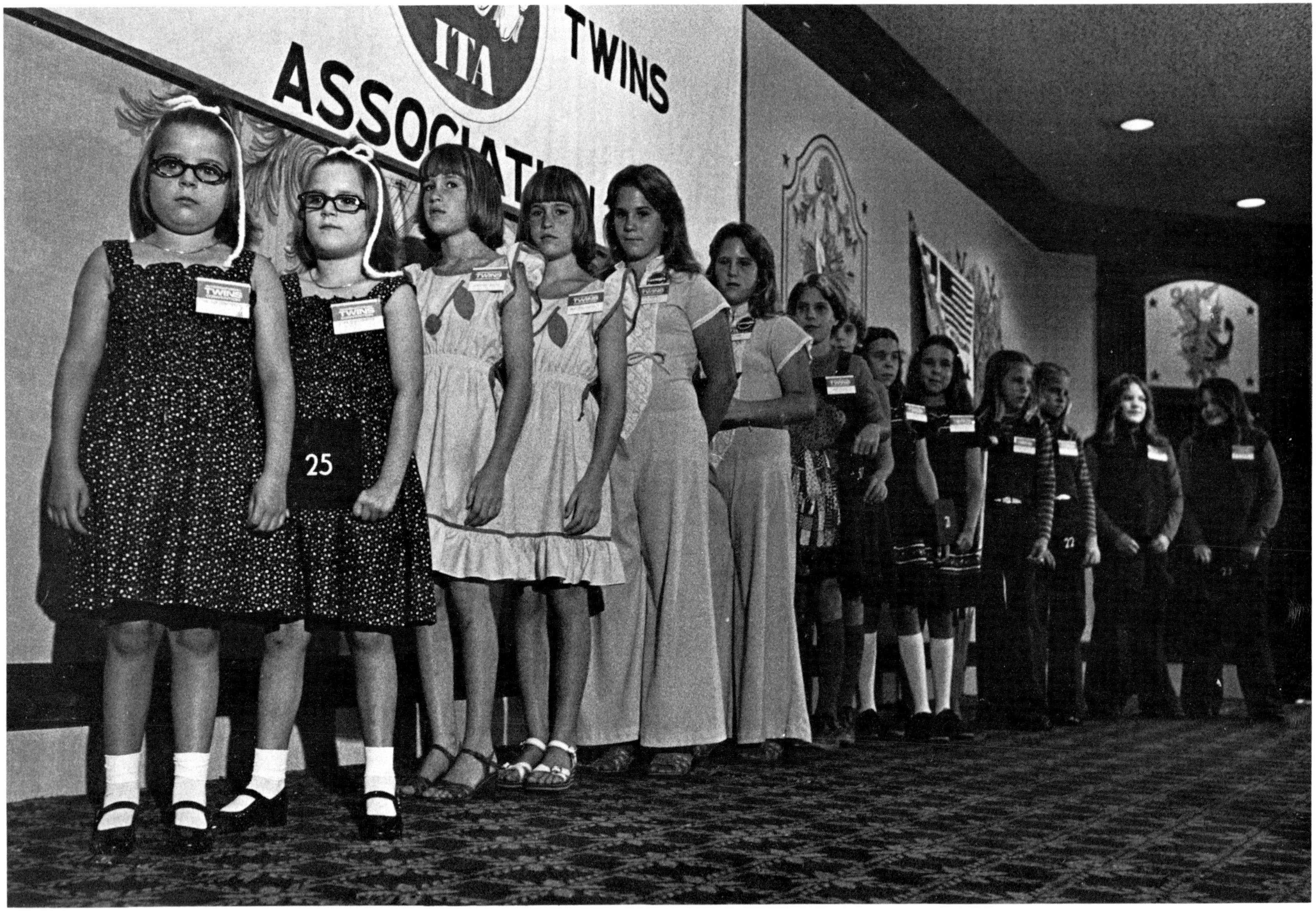

ITA
TWINS
ASSOCIATI
25

PARALLELS
A LOOK AT TWINS

Photographs by Harvey Stein
Text by TED WOLNER

E.P. DUTTON   NEW YORK

Photographs copyright © 1978 by Harvey Stein
Text Copyright © 1978 by Ted Wolner
All rights reserved. Printed in the U.S.A.

No part of this publication may be reproduced or transmitted in any form or by any means, electronic or mechanical, including photocopy, recording or any information storage and retrieval system now known or to be invented, without permission in writing from the publisher, except by a reviewer who wishes to quote brief passages in connection with a review written for inclusion in a magazine, newspaper or broadcast.

For information contact: E. P. Dutton, 2 Park Avenue, New York, N.Y. 10016

LIBRARY OF CONGRESS CATALOGING IN PUBLICATION DATA
Stein, Harvey.   Parallels.
Bibliograhy: p.
1. Twins—Psychology.   I. Wolner, Ted.   II. Title.
BF723.T9S74   1978   155.9′24   78-8662
ISBN: (cl) 0-525-17472-9   (pa) 0-525-04157-5

Published simultaneously in Canada by Clarke, Irwin & Company Limited, Toronto and Vancouver

DESIGNED BY ANN GOLD

10 9 8 7 6 5 4 3 2 1

First Edition

For Gertrude

For Louis, Grace and, especially, William Wolner

Author's Note

I am not a twin. But I am only thirteen months older than my sister and, when we were growing up, people would often say we looked just like twins. I'd think, how could that be? I had light hair and blue eyes; she had brown hair and brown eyes. No, I didn't think we looked alike. I didn't want to look like her; the thought greatly upset me.

I remember a pair of identical twins in my grade school, named Judy and Jody. They had the same wide gap between their front teeth, wore very thick glasses, and seemed always to be dressed in the same dark blue jumper with high socks and saddle shoes. I didn't know them well and was rather in awe of them. I did not understand how there could be two of one person and why I could rarely call them by their correct names. It was frightening sometimes.

During one weekend in May 1972, I met three sets of twins. Instantly struck by that coincidence (I hadn't seen twins in years), I became fascinated with the visual impact of their duplication, which aroused an extreme curiosity about their relationship. Intermittently over the next five and a half years, I interviewed and photographed more than 150 sets of twins, most of them identical and most of them people like the rest of us aside from the accident of their birth. I began to realize that, regardless of how alike identical twins appear to be, the camera can freeze their reality and allow us to see that there are differences between them. And these differences are often as fascinating as the similarities.

According to most twins, their twinship presents certain problems, the major one being the confusion of identity. It is difficult enough to learn and understand who you really are; for a twin, the difficulty is much greater. And similar names can only add to the confusion. The given names of the twins photographed for this book include: Leone and Ione, Dorothy and Dorris, Donald and Dennis, Colleen and Christine, Mitchell and Michael, Donna and Dianne, June and Jane, Beverly and Barbara, Darien and Daryl, Celia and Stella, Antonia and Antoinette, Ann Irene and Irene Ann, Rebecca and Roberta (nicknamed Becky and Bobby), Ronald and Donald, Bonnie and Connie, Randy and Candy, Bam Bam and Chi Chi.

I did not attempt to photograph the widest possible variety of twins; rather, I have concentrated on identical twins, whose relationships seemed emotionally the most intense and thus the most interesting. Most of the adult twins were quite sensitively aware of, and articulate about, their twinness, and I am grateful to them for being so open and honest with me, a stranger asking questions. The quotations that accompany the photographs in the book were gleaned from dozens of hours of interviews and taped conversations. They have been edited here and there for the sake of clarity, though such changes have been kept to a minimum. Rather more of a liberty has been taken with the placement of the quotations; in some cases they do not correspond to the specific pair of twins pictured on the facing page.

—Harvey Stein
New York City

PARALLELS
Text by Ted Wolner

Parallels
Becoming a Twin

In a brief essay written in 1909, Sigmund Freud described a cardinal episode in the psychic life of the child. Wholly encompassed by the environment his parents provide, the child inevitably identifies them as figures of incomparable qualities and incontestable power. Just as inevitably, the child's actual experience fails to conform to this idyllic family picture. Neither father nor mother always appears on demand; brothers and sisters too must share in a supply of parental love and care that in any event is limited; and some member of the family may actively do him injury. The child accumulates a series of experiences as a consequence of which he comes to feel fundamentally slighted. To mitigate this pain, the child then turns the energy of his resentment to the construction of imaginary replacements for his parents—to what Freud called "family romances."

Although the replacements he imagines are often parental figures, a frequent variation in the child's family romance is the fantasy of having an identical twin, whose functions for the child are several. The fantasized twin does exactly and only as the child wishes, offering all the love, attention, and companionship the child instinctively resents not having received from his parents. As in another variant of the family romance—the imaginary pet animal whose appeal is the consummate purity of its devotion—the child finds in his imaginary twin an understanding beyond even the need to speak. One man, an only child who became a father of real twins, recalled the fantasy twin of his childhood:

> We always got up together in the morning and greeted each other like lovers. When I had to go to school and pay attention to the teachers and the other children, I had my imaginary twin complain of his loneliness and then I would console him. We would take many walks in the woods together and it often seemed as if he wished to embrace me. Lying together in bed at night, his head between my arm and heart, he would softly utter a continuous purring, dreamlike murmur of complete bliss and contentment. This filled me with a quiet, almost religious warmth.

In a more aggressive fashion, the child may ascribe to the fantasy twin a reality he denies to his actual brothers, sisters, or parents. "No, you can't sit on that chair," he might declare with stubborn insistence. "My twin is sitting there." Through the imaginary twin–usurper, the child may enact his own version of a court intrigue against all rivals in the family for the center of attention. The child may also transfer his former idealization of his parents to the twin, endowing him with all the complementary traits and abilities the child feels a need for in himself. Or the two of them together, according to the child's magical way of thinking, may enter a whole new world of possibility, not unlike that in comic book versions of the super-hero.

When Clark Kent becomes Superman, the story line tells the child that the superhero is simply in secret disguise as an ordinary mortal. Psychically, however, the child may experience the double identity as two distinct, and complementary individuals—as twins in fact. Clark Kent's timid manner permits the child to identify the newspaper reporter with his own powerless self. Superman, as the twin of Clark Kent, employs powers beyond the compass of mortal men, thereby giving the child a supertwin with whom to identify his own fantasies of omnipotence.

The psychic movement of a child inventing a fantasy twin is the same as that required in the more passive, vicarious identification with an entire constellation of superheroes twinned to secret identities: Bruce Wayne–Batman, Dick Grayson–Robin, Billy Batson–Captain Marvel, Diana Prince–Wonder Woman. Such twinned pairs have no doubt relieved thousands of children of the need to create twin-heroes of their own. Both the child's fantasy of an omnipotent identical twin and his identification with the comic book superhero collapse the family romance to the self-sufficient union of an all-powerful twosome, a union shaped by the following formulation of the psyche: "I am unable to contest the control others have over me. If I were more clever and powerful, I would gloriously vindicate myself."

In all its variations, the fantasy of having a twin is fueled by a child's naturally large store of narcissism, the self-love that compensates for what is felt as a lack of love from others in the real world. According to Pausanias' version of the Narcissus myth, the youth who stared into a limpid pool until he pined away was actually attempting to recapture a lost twin sister out of his own reflection in the water. Thus he fell in love with himself as the image of her who so much resembled him. Similarly, a child, unconsoled for the inevitable separation from his parents, creates in the intense rush of wish fulfillment a twin that is an image of himself, and thereby dresses up self-love in the thin guise of love for another.

Although crucial differences ultimately separate the psychology of the single child and his imaginary twin from that of real identical twins, parallels and correspondences can be drawn between them which are nevertheless striking. Identical twins give each other an invaluable ally in reshaping the family romance, and they often function for each other in the same roles as the fantasized counterpart: inseparable companion, family usurper, complement, and hero. The narcissistic energies mobilized by the single child to generate an identical mate are also remarkably like the self-regarding stimuli that twins give each other. To this mutual attention is added the stimulation the twins as an entity receive from those around them.

We are, for instance, quick to find delight and entertainment in the sight of twin infants at play. Indistinguishable from one another, they flounder, exploring and climbing over each other with the innocence of animal cubs. The charm of such a scene is at odds with our own intensely held convictions regarding individuality: what charms us, in fact, is that these twins do not know just how *unindividual* they are. We marvel that an accident of birth can so nearly seem a conjurer's trick, as though a baby's mirror reflection were suddenly to crawl out from behind the glass and take on a life of its own.

We may speculate that in the minds of these twins the world is quite probably composed of nothing but an endless series of look-alikes—that if they could speak, they would ask us where *our* mates were. To play the amused audience to such a pair is at least momentarily to engage in the fantasy of having a twin ourselves. With their characteristic appeal, infant twins soothingly intimate that there is no need to struggle for identity should one possess so complete and immediate a replication of the self. Their charming collaborations gently mock the adult necessity of standing alone.

To the parents we may direct a predictable litany of observations and questions: "How delightful," "Amazing"; "How odd"; "What problems they must involve"; "Are they *completely* alike?" "Can you tell them apart?" "But how?" Hearing all this repeated throughout childhood and adolescence, twins come to feel their uniqueness as a unit, while the emotional charge they evoke as individuals separate from one another is distinctly less intense.

Compare for a moment the attention we give to twins with that we give to handicapped children. Marked by stigmata that are undeniable and permanent, they tempt us, in a rush of pity, to see them as less than fully human, to deny them any future or responsibility. A deformed child will inevitably feel pain at evoking these reactions. He must then adjust not only to his handicap but also to the image of himself as something to be intensely noticed, momentarily pitied, and then shunned—a kind of monster inescapably twinned to himself.

With twins, in contrast, there is no response we feel we have to censor, and so we envelop them in our own rapt attention. No less vividly than the handicapped child, however, twins acquire an image of themselves as others perceive them—as a pair rather than as two distinct individuals. Where the true individuality of a handicapped child tends to be hidden within the painful outer image of himself as a monster, the development of twins as individuals may be arrested by the pleasures of being perceived as a unit.

Other children unknowingly give twins this same encouragement. Dorothy Burlingham, a pioneer in the psychological analysis of twins, observed many instances of this. A three-and-a-half-year-old child saw her twin playmates, Margaret and Anne, in the garden, and called out, "Other Anne, other Anne, come here." Margaret did not answer. The child's calls grew louder and angrier. Asked why she did not call her Margaret, she answered, "Because she is another Anne." Other children often referred to Anne herself as "More Margaret." Upon seeing twin boys for the first time, one three-year-old child, Richard, immediately halted and stood pointing from one to the other saying, "Boy, boy," and then adding, "me not two Richies."

Quickly sensing that to be a twin is to have a readymade playmate or friend, children may feel jealous, left out, and at a disadvantage when confronted by the apparently ideal world inhabited by twins. Children's reactions to twins are also conditioned by their search for beings who resemble themselves. Parents' announcement that another child is on the way often stimulate children to imagine the baby-to-be as an identical being. School children often spontaneously make friends with others who have the same birthday or a similar name.

The first appearance in children's lives of real twins often comes as a kind of shock. Inevitably their reactions will be communicated to the twins in both obvious and subtle ways. As twins begin to see themselves possessing a tie of more than normal interest for other children and adults, there grows between them a bond that is in some ways superior to any other in a child's experience of relationships, whether with friends, brothers, sisters, or parents. The attention they receive together becomes a kind of sun around which their psyches tend increasingly to revolve.

The parents themselves have other reactions. The birth of a single child usually comes as a jolt into the anxious day-to-day reality of having to care for one helpless living thing. With the birth of twins, the jolt may easily be a plunge into temporary despair. One mother told Dorothy Burlingham in the course of the latter's researches, "I felt dismay that I should be inflicted with twins, when it was my first pregnancy and I should be single-handed." Another was herself very much pleased, but reported that her husband, because of the additional burdens of two infants, was "quite furious with me and refused to speak to me . . . He persisted [in saying] it must be all my fault and none of his." As Felicia Connors, a member of the National Organization of Mothers of Twins and past president of the New York State Association of Mothers of Twins Clubs, puts it, "Women who give birth to twins are [often] confronted with complex feelings of bewilderment, panic, even disgust." One mother told her of a more extreme reaction that many parents are more hesitant to express: "I was horrified and frightened to have twins. Somehow it was indecent."

Such reactions remind us that our own responses to twins are not always wholly innocent. A random event of cellular division, identical twins call to mind the somewhat uncomfortable knowledge that each of us is genetically very much an accident. In the presence of squirming, nursing infant twins, we may more easily associate their multiple needy movements with animal litters or insect larvae than with charming, helpless miniatures of adults. To observe a pair of twins is to see oneself for a moment as an instinctual organism, the product of a blind scheme in nature, thereby dispossessed of the dignity associated with more spiritual beings who somehow transcend their mere biology. The fact of twinning reduces the uniqueness, and thus the humanity, of each twin, and by extension all of us, for we too could have been the random cell that happened to subdivide. We ourselves might not have become the unique individuals we are so proud to suppose.

Yet twins may also stimulate in us deeper soundings of nature's mysteries. Identical twins occur when one cell, very soon after fertilization, splits off from the subdividing cluster of cells to plant itself on another side of the wall in the womb, there itself to subdivide and become a second foetus in nearly perfect parallel development with the first. The split, occurring with the same frequency across all the human races, happens for still undetermined reasons, making a twin nature's mysterious clone. In their absolutely exact cellular identity, twins hint at the trove of secrets abounding in the micro-universe of the cell with all its myriad discrete functions.

At birth, the labor of months, which is to be a life for years, finally comes to fruition. The unexpected arrival of two babies may bring a first and, then, a second bloom upon the richness of generation. In these double beings, how much more fulsome and teeming seems the power of life, how much more blind to all purpose and teleology except that of perpetuation. Twins intimate a cosmic tenacity, the refusal of organic life to slip back into the nothingness of inorganic matter. They help us see that we are but simple conduits in a process of creation vastly larger than ourselves.

They may also give us a heightened awareness of the vulnerability of life. Often born premature, twins force upon us the knowledge that they have inhabited crowded placental quarters for two in a womb which nature originally designed for the bearing of only one, that human life may not always pass through its terms of gestation completely free of injury or deprivation. After birth, still covered with gelatinous membrane, exposed to the sting of the air, twins wriggle with the awesome urgency of life, all the more poignant for there being two of them, paired in their spastic movements and helpless cries. Their double presence presses home the realization of what it might have meant for life to so struggle for issue and then, suddenly, not to survive.

Whether reacting to their arrival primarily with wonder or dismay, the parents invariably emphasize the similarity of twins, beginning with the assignment of alliterated names: Judy and Janet, Richard and Roger, David and Derek, Jill and Jane. Twins have also been cruelly named: Max and Climax, Kate and Duplicate, Romeo and Juliet, Ura and Ima Hog. Identical haircuts, inevitably identical clothes, and other actions foster the lockstep of twinship. Unexamined cultural attitudes—that identical twins also think and feel alike, rarely if ever fight, and have a closer relationship with one another than any other known to mankind—are so deeply ingrained that parents may take offense at any suggestion of dissimilarity in their twins, and will often refuse to acknowledge the logistical and psychological problems of handling two small infants at the same time. Under the pressure of these attitudes, the parents may convert their unacknowledged frustrations into subtle forms of rejection.

Burlingham observed that mothers frequently mistook one identical twin for the other, and also noted their mortification on discovering the error. The mothers felt as though they had showed an unpardonable lack of love. Indeed, many mothers find it difficult to love their twins until they can see differences between the two. In contrast, a single child automatically has his own individual nature—a smile, a scream, a flailing of the arms and legs, and his identity is established: he is *the baby*, unique to the family occasion. Identical twins, however, leave room for doubt about which one is to receive particular attention, or has already received it. If the exercise in discrimination becomes too difficult, or is too frequently necessary, the parents may lapse into treating the twins as a unit, experiencing their pleasures as parents on that basis alone. The twins in turn will sense their parents' response, and each may come to doubt that there is anything appealing about him as an individual. Moreover, the twins themselves inadvertently contribute to a lessening of their own individuality. The more parents and others tend to see each of them as only half of a whole, the more each will begin to see the company of the other as an entire universe.

It does not follow, however, that the interactions of twins are ones of infant harmony, for they often experience vast resentments toward one another. It is not exceptional for twins to fight each other in their carriage, as though it were a place too small to hold the two of them. A pair of twins observed by Burlingham began to act out their jealous antagonism at seventeen months. Because one twin repeatedly showed anger when the other received attention first, Bill and Bert were given separate, identical little tables at mealtime. On noticing that Bert was being fed first, Bill furiously threw his plate on the floor, all the while glowering at Bert. The violent desire to replace the other resembles the tantrums of a single child in every respect but one—that it tends to be directed against the twin rather than the parent. Where single children become accustomed to their own differences in ability as compared to older brothers and sisters, twins pass through the same developmental stages simultaneously, so that when one accomplishes some new skill ahead of his twin, the pain and frustration for the other are much greater.

Twins will sublimate a lot of these feelings into an activity common to all children—imitation. Twins may be found standing in their beds in the same position, or sucking each other's fingers, or moving in exactly the same way when they crawl, or rocking in the same rhythm while they hold onto the bars of their cribs—appearing as though shaped from a single piece of paper folded in half to produce two animated cut-outs. No one is better suited to the instant replay of imitation than twins, and together they will often create copying games, such as one recorded by Burlingham:

> At eleven months Bert clapped his hands and Bill did the same; he banged bricks on the table; Bill followed suit. These actions were always accompanied by laughter from both children. Soon it was impossible to tell who copied whom. One would start to shout and kick and the other would watch him and laugh; then the other would take his turn to shout and kick and the first one would watch and laugh.

There were times when neither their mother, nor other children who might have wished to join their antics, had any influence over them —their movements were characterized by ever wilder and more aggressive romping about the room. Twins sometimes appear to be a conspiracy of two against their parents and other children, a union of something wholly foreign and delinquent, their taunts and provocations against the world outside themselves a precocious mastery of evil. At such moments, twins seem almost monstrously possessed of skills we usually associate only with adults—the skills of extensive collaboration and collusion.

When one twin expresses a strong emotion, the other twin will often be affected by it, instantaneously grafting it onto himself and reflecting it in identical behavior. Madge, one of another set of twins, fell down in some gravel and hurt herself, thus gaining a lot of affectionate attention from her mother. Seconds later, her twin, Mary, sensing the cause of this maternal affection, purposely fell down too, cut herself and began screaming. "As soon as one got hurt," their mother said, "I'd give the other one attention too. I had to catch on fast. They were getting hurt a lot."

Similar to this contagion of mood, twins will often develop an emotional and functional division of labor, bringing complementary characteristics and feelings into play with one another. The more active twin may exhibit dominant, aggressive, and selfish traits, and the passive twin become gentler and more submissive. Twins may switch active–passive, dominant–submissive roles with some frequency throughout their early years. In these exchanges, twins may become so practiced as to appear interchangeable. Another set of twin girls would take turns crying whenever the mother left the house. When the mother finally asked who was not making a fuss, and why, she was told, "Sister's crying. I don't need to." The relative passivity of one twin may be due to disparities in strength to which premature twins are particularly subject. More frequently, though, the passivity is entirely accidental. One twin, having suddenly discovered that he can push his mate away from a prized toy, proceeds to generalize this knowledge into other behavior with his twin, in the manner of the first primate to use a stick originally as a lever and then as a weapon. Passivity may be imposed on one twin through a momentarily greater involvement by the other in some activity. Or in the cycles of development, one twin may temporarily overtake the other in strength.

If, however, one twin consistently dominates, the submissive twin's creative impulses will all be stillborn. Nor will the dominant one escape the pull of a subtle mutual dependency, for just as the passive twin is caught in the slavish compulsion to model his behavior on that of his mate, so the active one becomes accustomed to the pleasures of watching the reactions he produces in his twin. The psychic division of labor between them may be such that together they represent a single personality, a kind of jigsaw interlock whose indentations and projections are irregular but perfectly meshed.

For a single child, there is often a phase during which talking to oneself is sufficiently pleasurable to overcome any desire to communicate with others. With twins, a constantly present other self makes such closed circuit communication not simply enjoyable but exciting. Like the nymph Echo of Greek mythology, who pined after Narcissus, one twin will tend to repeat whatever is said by the other, to such a degree that twins will frequently develop whole glossaries of nonsense syllables which they alone understand.

The development of language in twins is often temporarily retarded by the self-absorbed communications of this echolalia. In a well-known study by Irene Lezine, children at the age of twenty-four months were asked to say their own names. Only forty percent of the twins could, compared to sixty percent among children who were not twins. At the same age, in a second test, children were asked to point to parts of their own body and then identify them on a picture. Forty-two percent of the twins passed, again lagging behind the sixty percent in the non-twin control group. One child would answer when the name of his twin was called. Another pointed to parts of his twin's body instead of his own. When still another twin momentarily lost her identification bracelet, she became unsure whether she was herself or her sister. Other tests have shown that twins improve their language development to age level when separated.

Twins may also suffer from what amounts to a kind of benign parental neglect: twins tend to receive shorter hugs, less praise, and fewer reprimands than singly born children. Because their parents assume that twins can amuse each other, they more often leave their twins alone than do parents of single children. Thus, twins may temporarily fall behind in language development much as a single child may become autistic when severely deprived of opportunities for relating to other people.

For many single children, it may be some time after their first gaze into a mirror before they recognize themselves, and still later that they begin to pat and kiss their own reflections, like infant versions of Narcissus. Twins, however, almost invariably take the image to be that of the person most familiar to them, namely the twin. At two years and five months, Bill customarily spoke of Bert, his twin, as "other one Bill"—an instance of Bill's more dominant nature. On seeing his own reflection in the lavatory mirror while urinating, he said, "Other one Bill do wee-wee." At twenty-two months, just as she was beginning to speak, Jessie looked extremely pleased on seeing her reflection, pointed at it and said, "Bessie," the name of her twin sister.

For a single child, acquaintance with his mirror image is a first act of self-consciousness, a rudimentary proof of existence. For a twin, however, the process of identifying the mirror image as his twin may well facilitate a loss of self-definition. Although he naturally learns that mirror reflections are just that, he may nevertheless maintain for years a sense that another person of independent life, his twin, accompanies him in his moments in front of the mirror. Indeed, he may often bypass the mirror itself and turn to his twin to see how he looks in his latest set of identical clothes.

Because of their overidentification with one another, twins often find even a brief separation from each other a difficult experience. At the age of four, Jessie caught scarlet fever and was confined in a hospital away from the nursery. For the first week Bessie was in great distress, constantly crying, "I want my Jessie, I want my sister." She continuously inspected herself for the red spots symptomatic of the fever. Whenever she found even a minute red spot, she would say, "I got it now, I must go to the hospital." Throughout the first days of their separation, Bessie stopped laughing entirely, ate very little, withdrew from playmates, and played in front of the mirror, as if the reflection were Jessie. She began to draw messages for Jessie, and to keep chocolates, pictures, and other gifts for her sister stored in envelopes on her table. For these she invented the term "embilance," coined from "envelope" and "ambulance." During bath time, she asked why there was no towel on Jessie's rack.

As Burlingham observed, Bessie's behavior resembled in all its particulars that of an adult in mourning, whose common characteristics are bereavement, loneliness, withdrawal from others, overestimation of the qualities of the loved one, and even temporary denials of reality.

Separation, if long enough, may also provide an occasion for the release of other more antagonistic emotions. Madge and Mary, another set of twins Burlingham studied, were separated while Madge spent seven months in the hospital. After her twin's return, Mary showed great anger and jealousy over now having to share their mother's affection with Madge. One day soon after her return, Madge was found rocking and screaming on the floor, an ugly blue mark on her forehead where Mary had hit and punched her. Mary continued theatening her in a low voice: "I shall go on hurting you. You are a big job, wee wee." When Madge shouted in reply, "No, you are," Mary picked up some stones and threw them at her sister. "You should stay in the hospital," Mary yelled. "You are a shitty bum, I will tell everybody they shouldn't like you."

When peers conflict, they have more at stake than other contestants; nothing is given or granted either, since by definition they are so equally matched. But the status of real peers, of two who emerge from distinct backgrounds, does not depend—as it does for twins—upon their absolute identity. Rather, it grows out of the sense that they are both equal to the occasion of their encounter. What each possesses is a comparable mastery of experience, however much their particular experiences may differ. Whether in cooperation or in conflict, peers maintain a sense of their own distinctive boundaries as individuals, unhindered by the intense identification with one another that is experienced by twins. There is between peers a necessary distance which for twins has never existed. Although they are equals, it cannot be said that twins are peers.

Indeed, fights like the one between Mary and Madge are exceptional. Much more often, the discharge of such aggressive feelings will be checked by twins through an overextended act of empathy. Aggression past a certain point of tolerance poses for twins a threat of a particular kind—the pain of a separation that they will experience as an amputation of the self. To negotiate the conflicting needs to compete and cooperate, twins will curb larger aggressions and together declare a truce. The effect, as with most truces, will be to suspend hostilities, while leaving them fundamentally unresolved. Unlike the parties to most such agreements, however, twins will rarely if ever break them.

There are powerful incentives for twins to keep the peace. A single child's unabashed seeking of praise or admiration is generally directed toward the adult world, with occasional efforts to impress younger brothers and sisters or to curry the favor of older ones. A twin, however, soon learns to seek approval for looks, clothing, and achievements from his twin at least as often as from parents. Twins also learn early to display one another to other people. Bessie once showed off Jessie in a new dressing gown, saying, "Look, look," to many adults and children who were gathered in the room. In thus exhibiting each other, the twins are imitating the behavior of their parents who often put them on display. Both receive gratification for the show over which they mutually preside, empresarios aborning.

When Jessie and Bessie began their toilet training, each would inspect the other's pot and praise her for success. An intimacy that extends even to moving their bowels is vivid proof that twins give over to one another the roles more often reserved for parents. Similarly, whenever either Bessie or Jessie observed that her sister had misbehaved in some way, that twin would immediately say, "No, no," to the other. Each served for her twin as a kind of behavioral conditioner, a surrogate conscience or parent-figure urging more proper deportment.

The dependent single child, accustomed to having everything given to him on demand, cannot empathize with another point of view because he is so preoccupied with his own. Twins, however, as they sense other people's deference to their union, are accordingly much more inclined to nourish an infant altruism, as in acts of comforting one another. When Jessie fell down and her nose started to bleed, Bessie responded by crying in sympathy, then stroking her, and finally, after her nose stopped bleeding, smiling and saying, "Jessie better." The affection many twins are so willing to give one another are the same expressions of love which parents give their children, and which twins incorporate to further embellish their rich emotional world.

Yet much of the altruism of twins is underwritten by a rigid, literal notion of what fairness means. On their second birthday, Jessie gave a very clear demonstration of this psychology. In front of the table where their mother had placed presents of a book, a toy dog, and a frock, Jessie checked off each of the gifts one by one to make sure they were equal: "Bessie doggie, Jessie doggie, Bessie book, Jessie book, Bessie dress, Jessie dress."

In the course of her researches, Burlingham

received many letters and statements from mothers of twins about the tenacity with which twins hold to this psychology of fairness. "In my experience," wrote one mother, "the twins themselves virtually dictate to you how to treat them; at the moment we have to dress them alike (twenty months) and give them identical toys because they are so very apt to be envious of the other's possessions. And I don't think they are able yet to understand that their own thing, though different, may be as valuable as the thing the sister has." Nowhere is the campaign against differences more concentrated than in the area of clothes, the most emblematic manifestation of the identical nature of twins. Twins sense that they, more than other people, are what they wear. An attempt to dress them differently will literally produce an identity crisis.

This psychology is the long-term product of an infant's wish to have everything. As soon as one twin recognizes the other as a rival, he recasts this wish in terms of the unavoidable competition. As part of their truce limiting hostilities toward one another, each begins to renounce demands on the condition that a corresponding renunciation is extracted from the twin; separate but equal possessions becomes the psychic imperative. The parental insistence that the twins share equally, which they once accepted passively, is now transformed by them into the active demand for equal treatment by others. Any transgression of this strict code by one twin, however unintentional, will precipitate immediate and possibly even violent conflict. Once the rule has been fully established, however, twins will consistently behave toward one another with genuine altruism, including the defense of one another in fights with outsiders.

During their first four years together, throughout the innumerable and minute negotiations of their everyday life, twins will generally construct a relationship whose satisfactions parallel with almost complete fidelity the functions performed by an imaginary twin for a lonely or misunderstood single child. Each twin finds in the other the inseparable companion whose mutual warmth, security, comfort, and help are insulation against those moments when parents are unavailable, indifferent, or even actively hostile. Their perfectly tuned sensitivities will discern and respond to subtle cues from one another, signals so slight that to others they appear telepathic. In this, the twins are as close to each other as any two persons who have refined their responses to one another throughout the term of an active and sustained intimacy.

Like the single child's imaginary double, twins will form themselves into a complementary team. Each will take advantage of whatever unique qualities of temperament the other one may possess. A greater patience in one twin gives both the rewards of whatever activities require fine tuning. The greater impulsiveness of the other ties them both more vitally to the concern of the moment. In their indissoluble commune of two, they trade off the absolute will of the single individual for a mutual curb on the natural imperialism of the psyche, their antagonisms receding into the background of the unconscious.

As each continues to focus, embody, and act out a family romance through the person of his twin, the heightened satisfactions of fantasy life, so much like those of an imaginary double for a single child, become incarnate for twins as the vivid reality of someone more nearly like himself than anyone he will ever again encounter. Individually, however, they may exhibit a poverty of self outside the emotional plenitude of their relations together, an overdependence and an overidentification with one another that will make it more and more difficult for them to separate, and to transfer their affections to people not included in their intense world of two.

Oppositions
Twins in Ritual and Myth

The double response of many parents to their twins, a reaction which mingles joy with disgust, parallels in a less extreme way the responses of ancient and aboriginal peoples to twins. In these societies, from antiquity to modern times, the most pronounced response has been to regard twins as unnatural and monstrous, as a violation of the cosmic order which is likely to call down upon an entire people fierce retribution from the local deities.

Among several tribal groups of the Niger Delta in West Africa, the mother of twins is either killed or made an outcast. The outcast mothers often die of hunger and exposure, or take their own lives in despair. A slave woman is assigned the task of killing the twins themselves. She takes each child by the ankles and the neck and breaks its back across her knees. She then places the twins in a pot, which she takes into the forest, where its contents are devoured by animals and insects. In certain areas of Dahomey, twins used to be thrown into water and drowned immediately, the mother was impaled, and her breasts were cut off.

The people of West Nias in the Indonesian archipelago believed twins would become murderers and poisoners if allowed to live. One or both of the twins would be hung from a tree in a sack, there to perish miserably. The Antambahoaka people of Madagascar put twins to death because they believed that twins would either die or go mad and try to kill their parents. To the Maidu Indians, who once inhabited the western slopes of the northern California sierra, twins were an exceptionally bad omen, and consequently were buried alive or burned to death along with their mother. Among the Hottentots, a male about to be married will amputate one of his testicles to prevent the birth of twins.

Before the period of British rule, the Bavenda tribes of the northern Transvaal in southeastern Africa killed twins by strangling or scalding them. Among some Ambo groups in southwestern Africa, twins are held to be unclean, and are killed immediately after birth by stuffing dirt into their mouths to suffocate them. As a purification, the mother must be shaved all over her body with a blunt razor in such a way that gashes are cut and blood flows freely, so as to rid her of the blood that has gone bad because of having had twins in her womb.

In many places, what were originally the severest proscriptions against twins have subsequently been modified. The Bassari of Togoland will preserve the boy when the twins are of both sexes, or the stronger of the two when they are of the same sex. The Kafirs regard twins as scarcely human and will taunt the mother of twins as one in disgrace, but they do not kill twins, who were once believed to be exceptionally savage and courageous, and were thus singled out to lead a military attack.

Among some tribes of the Thonga, a woman who gives birth to twins may speak to no one, and is removed to a shelter outside the village. To purify herself, the woman must pass along her defilement by having incomplete sexual intercourse with four men in succession; the first three of these will die as a consequence. Following the fourth such act, she undergoes special vapor baths and returns to her parents' home. Here she entertains yet another lover, by whom she must conceive a child, and thus complete the purification.

In South Africa, the Herero believe the birth of twins to be "the greatest and most fortunate event which can happen to a mortal Omuherero." Yet the parents of twins immediately fall under a taboo. Their clothes are taken from them in return for worthless skins, and they are temporarily ejected from the village. All villagers and their cattle must gather in the village or be bewitched and die. When the father of the twins returns to greet everyone, the villagers receive him as an enemy, throwing different kinds of missiles at him while the women raise a ceremonial lamentation. Over the next month or more, the twins' father is given gifts of meat or of live cattle as he goes walking through his own and neighboring villages. He has now become a privileged being, with the right to represent the chief of the village and perform priestly functions. The twins themselves, if they are boys, automatically inherit the same sacred privileges. Here the taboo on the parents and twins makes them sacred, not accursed. Like those who put twins to death, however, these people see twins as equivocal and uncanny beings. The gifts to the father and the rituals of which he is the focus serve to deflect the curse from the community and to restore normal relations, thus integrating the sacred twin infants into ordinary life.

Many groups in Thailand and the Malay Peninsula consider the advent of twins a very lucky occurrence, but the close emotional connection between the twins is regarded as dangerous. If misfortune strikes one, it is believed that the other will also die. Thus, various peoples of Africa, the Ainu of Japan, several societies in the central provinces of India, the Philippine Islands, and parts of Micronesia separate twins from one another, placing them in different families, or they observe other rites to break the special sympathy between twins.

Even the very few groups who appear in no way to regard the birth of twins as anomalous, do nevertheless express some underlying fears concerning them. The Shuswap, who occupy portions of the Fraser and Columbia River basins in British Columbia, hold twins to be "a great mystery," and their birth a most fortunate event. Still, the parents must shift their own camp from the village to the woods, even if the birth occurs in midwinter, and are not allowed near other people for four years. Every day the mother or father must wash and scour the twins with fir branches.

For the Dogon of Africa, twins represent a perfect androgynous union. The Dogon adorn their marketplaces with shrines of stone or clay dedicated to twins, whom they believe to be the inventors of trade and economic reciprocity. They see in twins a fundamental binary attraction, symbolic of such social bonds as those between buyer and seller, husband and wife, a man and his best friend, rich and poor, a man and his shadow, a man and his placenta, partners in commerce, or a host and a stranger. Any Dogon child born singly is immediately linked to an animal that represents the child's unborn twin. The idea of twins so permeates every aspect of the Dogon social structure that uncanny fears have been displaced onto everything not identifiable with twins.

Where twins survive, aboriginal peoples principally ascribe to them powers to control the weather and promote the fertility of land, beast, men and women. The Shuswap believe it will rain when a twin bathes in a lake or river. In the central provinces of India, one of a pair of twins prevents injuries to crops from excessive rainfall, hailstorm, or wind by painting his right buttock black and the left buttock whatever color he chooses, and then standing flush with the direction of the wind. In South Africa, the Bathonga bring rain by having women strip naked and go in procession, led by the mothers of twins, to the graves of twins or of an abortion. There they may pour water on the graves, or they may disinter the remains and re-bury them in mud near water. In some regions of East Africa, a twin about to cross a stream or a river, or one crossing a lake in a storm, protects himself and his fellow travelers by filling his mouth with water, spurting it out, and saying, "I am a twin."

The Yuman Indians of Colorado believe twins are descended from heaven to add to the fertility of crops through their rain-making ability. Twins of the same sex are dressed identically in red, white, and black, the colors of the clouds. Yuman twins demand special and equal gifts so that "they will remain awhile" on earth, a custom which arouses envy among other Yuman not so specially treated. The llama-raisers in Peru during the time of the Incas also took twins as a token of fertility, calling the twins of both llamas and humans "children of lightning," and the wind "the breath of twins."

Among aboriginal peoples of the world, until very recently, there appeared to be no distinction made between fraternal and identical twins. The sheer phenomenon of two beings born at the same time, along with the benign or evil powers ascribed to them, apparently combine to render unimaginable any functional distinction between those twins who look exactly alike and those who do not. However, a distinction is often drawn between twins of the same sex and those whose sex is mixed. Throughout the Old World from Africa to Micronesia, mixed-sex twins are often said to have had intercourse while still in the womb. This is sometimes permitted in royal families—especially those where royalty is divinely ordained—but in commoners it is considered the most heinous form of incest, an occasion which usually calls for the immediate killing of the twins. Yet many New World Indians consider twins of mixed sex to have been married in some former life; others have viewed them as a divine couple uncontaminated by sexuality.

Many aboriginal peoples believe it is impossible for a father to beget more than one child at a time, leading to suspicions that the second-born child is the result of adultery by the mother, a belief which, as among the Hottentots, quickly leads to ending the life of the twins. Or the paternity of twins may be ascribed to eating a double fruit, such as two bananas grown from one stem. The Zulus do not eat objects of food in pairs, nor do they receive two articles simultaneously from the hands of another for fear they may beget twins. More often, however, twins are seen as the result of impregnation by good or evil spirits or by a god.

Our own response to this astonishing variety of beliefs, ritual murders and ceremonial purifications associated with twins parallels in a smaller way the responses to twins of aboriginal peoples themselves. For them, twins figure as the sudden eruption into everyday life of a supernatural order of things. The many societies which associate twins with rain and storms—like the Peruvians who called twins "the children of lightning" and the wind "the breath of twins"—must surely identify lightning as the visible and thunder as the aural representations of the experience of witnessing the birth of twins, of two who possess preternatural powers. Storms render the mood of this event, become the resonant symbol of the additional suffering of a mother who brings forth two instead of one, become the naturalistic image of the profound shock, as of a transcendent event, which the appearance of twins registers in the aboriginal imagination.

Ritual momentarily captures, concentrates, and expresses through a rigorously defined composition of actions and invocations all the power of an individual belief. Ritual hints at larger mysteries which remain unexplored beyond the outline known to all who practice the highly schematized ceremonies. Over time, however, a ritual's suggestive power is filled out and realized in the narratives of an oral tradition, becoming a fully articulated series of interlocking tales, a whole mythology, as if several documentary films had been teased and coaxed from out of the story suggested by a single photograph.

In the myths that grow out of rituals, such as the ones just discussed, twin figures are often pivotal. According to the origin myth of the Iroquois, the woman Ataensic fell through a rift in the sky. Pregnant, she soon gave birth to a daughter—who then mysteriously became pregnant herself with twin boys, Iosekha and Tawiscara. Being of an evil nature, Tawiscara refused to be born in the natural fashion, breaking his way upward from the womb and through one side, below his mother's armpit, thus ending her life. When his brother Iosekha moved to provide the new and still arid earth with life-giving water, Tawiscara created a giant frog to drink it all up.

A fight ensued in which Iosekha drove his brother to the extreme west. Tawiscara bled at each step, and the blood turned to barren flint. Iosekha then established his lodge in the far east, and opened a cave in the earth. From it he brought forth all the land animals; then he formed men and instructed them in the arts of making fire, growing corn, and imparting fertility to the soil. This theme is repeated in many of the myths of North and South American Indians. A primeval woman breaks a taboo and gives birth to twins, who become warriors, heroes, and medicine men. Usually the elder twin is the hero and giver of culture, and the younger one the source of evil, the twin who is ultimately condemned to outer darkness.

In contrast, the Bakairi of the Amazon basin believe that the mother of their race was once a captive of the jaguars. She became pregnant with twins by sucking two finger bones of Bakairi who had been killed by these same animals, and she died before giving birth. The still living twins, Keri and Kame, were cut from her body and fostered by the jaguars. The twins did not yet have a fully human form, but manipulated one another until each was complete. They then avenged their mother's death on the jaguars, procured the sun and the moon with the help of the vultures, stole fire from the fox, and obtained water from the snake to make the rivers. From other animals, Keri and Kame got hammocks, arrows, tobacco, manioc, cotton, stones for houses, and even sleep. They invented flutes and dancing, created several tribes of men, quarreled but made up their dispute, and finally disappeared without a trace.

The most elaborate origin myths involving twins are those of the ancient Egyptians. Ra, the first god of the universe, created another four—two sets of twins.

From the union of one of these pairs came four children: Osiris, Set, Isis, and Nephthys, whose fates are also interwoven around themes common to twins. Osiris, in the many legends surrounding him, appears variously as the husband of Isis who is sometimes her elder brother, and at other times her twin. The first civilizer of Egypt, Osiris fashioned the implements and techniques of agriculture. By skill and gentleness alone, he subjugated country after country throughout the known world, while Isis governed Egypt, keeping the kingdom in perfect order.

But his younger brother Set became intensely jealous of Osiris, and conspired with seventy-two others to murder him and lock his body inside a coffer which he cast into the Nile. Carried by the river, it floated into the Mediterranean and found its way to the Phoenician coast. Isis, overwhelmed with grief, cut off her hair, tore her robes, and went in search of the coffer. Having at last found it, she hid it in the swamps of Buto, where Set came upon it by accident. To annihilate Osiris forever, he cut the body into fourteen pieces and scattered them in all directions. Isis went in search of the precious fragments until she had reconstituted her brother's body—except for his phallus, which was never found. She then performed embalming rites which miraculously restored the murdered god to life.

In this, she was assisted by Nephthys, her twin sister and the wife of Set, who had left him immediately on hearing of his crime. Isis and Nephthys, one of the few pairs of female twins to figure in any pantheon, alternated with each other in the funeral lamentations for Osiris. The creator of the embalming rites was Anubis. Since she had no children by Set, Nephthys had once made Osiris drunk and drawn him into her arms. Osiris made love to her thinking she was Isis, and of their union was born Anubis. Also present at the funeral rites was the child Horus, born miraculously to Isis out of a union with Osiris' posthumously reanimated corpse. Variously described as the "twin" of his father Osiris, and as his literal reincarnation, Horus eventually avenged his father's death by attacking Set, savagely cutting his body into many pieces. Resurrected, Osiris could have regained his throne as king of Egypt and reigned over the living, but he preferred to rule over the Kingdom of the Dead, where he warmly welcomed the souls of the just.

According to most interpretations of these myths, Osiris represents the spirit of vegetation, which annually dies and is then reborn. The struggle between Set and Osiris is the struggle between the desert and the fertile earth, between the drying wind and the vegetation, aridity and fecundity, darkness and light. Isis represents the rich plains of Egypt, which are made fertile each year by the annual inundations of the Nile (Osiris). Because of her fearless travels in search of the body of Osiris, she was also known as the star of the sea, the patroness of travelers, and the wife and mother of the sun. Nephthys, her twin, represents the desert's edge, whose barrenness occasionally becomes fruitful due to high spring flooding by the Nile. On coffin lids and on the interior walls of sarcophagi, these twins are often depicted as identical spirits with wings outstretched in a gesture of protection over the dead.

Twins also appear in myth as the builders of nations and cities, seldom without intense and bitter rivalry between the brothers. Their prototype for the Western world is the story of Jacob and Esau. According to Talmudic lore, their rivalry began in the womb, where it gave such pain to Rebecca that by the seventh month of pregnancy she regretted having had the curse of childlessness removed. With each of the twins determined to be first to enter the world and claim the vaunted birthright, it was only when Esau threatened to prevail at the expense of his mother's life that Jacob gave way. On reaching manhood, the weaker-willed Esau was persuaded by Jacob to sell his birthright for a bowl of lentil stew to satisfy his hunger; and Jacob, disguising himself as the hairier Esau, received his blind father's blessing and went forth to found the nation of Israel.

In Greek mythology, the twins Amphion and Zethus built Thebes without any such antagonism. Amphion was the more powerful, however, the muses having given him a lyre that could charm the stones themselves into joining; thus were built the palace and the city walls of Thebes.

Among city-founders the most famous twins are, of course, Romulus and Remus. Sired by Mars, the god of war, when he lay with a sleeping Vestal virgin, the newborn twins were put into a basket and set afloat on the Tiber. Washed ashore, they were found and suckled by a she-wolf, and later reared by a shepherd and his wife. While they were marking out the foundations of the city that was to be Rome, Remus mocked Romulus and jumped over the wall his brother had begun to build. They quarreled; Remus was killed, and Romulus thus became the city's ruler and consolidated the power of the Roman state. Mars now asked Jove for permission to bring Romulus, his only son, to the home of the immortal gods. Jove consented, covering the sky with clouds and making the earth tremble with thunder and lightning while Romulus was carried off to join the immortals. Renamed Quirinus, he became the patron deity of Rome.

The rivalries of Iosekha and Tawiscara, Romulus and Remus, Jacob and Esau, and even of Osiris and Set, suggest that no city wall or national boundary would ever safely stand without the spilling of blood, without continuous fratricidal struggle. Indeed, upon murdering his brother, Romulus declared, "So perish whoever else shall leap over my battlements." In their agonistic settings, the twin brothers illustrate the innate tendency of the human psyche to contrast, to echo, to balance, to oppose. These antagonistic twins function as a kind of ultimate dramatic nemesis, as if unknowingly they were accomplices who could not resist meeting. Conversely, Osiris and Isis, Isis and Nephthys, Horus and Osiris, the

Dogon spirit world of twins, and many other twin cosmologies all suggest a once-broken, embryonic unity seeking reconstitution, a devotion to the twin brother or twin sister as large as the cosmos itself, a kind of metaphysical sublimation of the ancient desire for a perfect union with another.

This theme is most pronounced in the set of myths that depict twins as heroes, of which the archetype is the legend of the Greek brothers, Castor and Pollux. Zeus, in one of his frequent amours, disguised himself as a swan and thus seduced the mortal Leda. She was delivered of two eggs, one of which contained Pollux and Helen and the other Castor and Clytemnestra. Following the aboriginal belief that twins are the issue of adultery, Caster was said to be the mortal son of Leda's husband Tyndareus, king of Sparta, and Pollux to be the son of Zeus, and thus immortal. And the creation at once of the immortal Helen, whose abduction launched the Trojan War, and the mortal Clytemnestra, whose revenge for the sacrifice of her daughter precipitated the events that are a major theme of Greek tragedy, suggest the pivotal importance of twinship for the ancient Greeks.

Castor and Pollux, traveling with Jason aboard the ship *Argo* in search of the Golden Fleece, calmed the waters during a terrible storm. As among so many aboriginal peoples, the power of twins is here once again identified with thunder and lightning. Two flames then descended from the sky and hovered about the heads of Castor and Pollux as a sign of their power over the elements, the sea-tossed epiphany of demi-gods who were the protectors of life. Electrical charges striking the masts and yards of a vessel during storms on the Mediterranean were said by the ancients to be manifestations of the twins.

As patrons of the kings of Sparta, Castor and Pollux would appear in battle, mounted on magnificent milk-white steeds and bearing lances whose metal tips gave off flashes of keen light—divine spearmen who gave their allies the edge they needed for victory, as among the African Kafirs who placed twins on the front line of war.

In the last of their battles, Castor was mortally wounded. Pollux, as an immortal, could not follow Castor to Hades, the region of the dead, and wept with grief at the separation. Zeus, touched by his grief, then granted Castor the privilege of immortality. The twins were permitted to live together, alternating a day in Hades with one among the immortal gods. Finally their inseparability was consecrated by a fixed position among the stars, where they became known as the Gemini or Dioscuri, the sons of the gods. The Greeks venerated the Dioscuri for centuries as tutelary divinities of warriors and sailors, and of travelers in general. They inspired religious cults throughout Asia Minor, the Middle East, and all over Europe.

They are closely resembled by the Asvins of the *Rig-Veda*. Like the Dioscuri, these figures of East Indian mythology are identified as horsemen and miracle-workers. Their inseparability is often compared to that of the eyes or the hands. They cause rain to fall and the earth to become fertile. They rescue the shipwrecked from the ocean and heal the wounds of those fallen in battle. The Asvins' epiphany of light and flame is the daily yoking of their chariot, which gives birth to the dawn.

Like Osiris, who ruled first over the living and then over the dead, and like the Gemini, who spent one day and night in Hades and the next with the gods, the Asvins are a link between mortality and everlasting life, expiring at night with the sun to be reborn again at daybreak, in an eternal cycle of death and rebirth. They represent pre-Christian hopes of immortality, are prefigurations of a Christian resurrection of all souls from the dead. The twin-hero romance, running through the Osirian, Dioscuric and Asvin traditions, survives in modern times in the fantasies of single or lonely children who imagine all-powerful companions for themselves, and in the debased form of the comic-book super-hero, whose functions as twins have already been discussed.

In most of these mythological tales, the fears which twins stimulate among aboriginal peoples exert little influence. The universe of these mythologies rests on beliefs to which no one any longer grants a literal reality. There are nevertheless traces of the fearful and the ambivalent which attach themselves to the anomalous births and the seemingly impossible tasks assigned to mythological twins. Both these features are most clearly represented in the life of Hercules, a heroic twin fathered by Zeus.

Desiring the mortal Alcmena, Zeus made himself the exact double of her husband, Amphitryon. Mistakenly having lain with Zeus-Amphitryon, Alcmena became pregnant with the demi-god Hercules and the wholly mortal Iphicles. At term, she endured a labor of seven torturous days and seven horrid nights, inflicted upon her by the vengeful wrath of Zeus' wife, Hera. Later, much as the Dioscuri had to go off in search of the Golden Fleece, Hercules was forced to do battle against mythological creatures which suggest the more monstrous associations attached to all multiple births: Cerberus, the three-headed dog of Hades; the hydra-serpent of nine heads, which grew a new head for every one lopped off; Nessus, the double-bodied monster of much swiftness, strength and violence, whose encounter with Hercules occurred near the spot where Romulus founded Rome.

Similarly, it is at least vaguely repulsive to find that Romulus and Remus were conceived by a god of war who lay with a sleeping virgin, or that Tawiscara murdered his mother with his own violent birth out of her side and armpit, or that Esau so mightily wished to claim his birthright that he too would have sacrificed his mother's life in birth. Many North and South American Indians believe that the original twins were born in punishment of a divine woman who broke a taboo and died in giving them life. Several pairs of mythological twins—Hercules, Romulus and Remus, Iosekha and Tawiscara, Keri and Kame, and others—are orphaned soon after birth, perhaps a vestigial reminder in these myths that twins were not always unequivocally welcomed by the peoples who originated their stories. In all these anomalies, twin births are connected with the monstrous as well as the divine.

Parallels and Oppositions
Twins and the Uncanny

For the ancient peoples who created mythologies focused on them, and for aboriginal peoples who still hold to beliefs about their divine or demonic status, twins represent a form of the uncanny, of something fearful which at the same time cannot be easily described or comprehended. Historically, the phenomenon of twins has provoked among these peoples contradictory interpretations which seem to defy any attempt at reconciliation. In some aboriginal societies, twins seem to be infant *deus ex machina,* self-creating, self-sustaining gods, human representations of a deity's fundamental qualities. It is only a small step from this impression to associating twins with the life-giving properties of waters, storms, fertile ground and the cycles of nature. To other peoples, however, it is this same impression which frequently leads to the immediate slaughter of twins. For they are usually perceived as two equal beings in aboriginal societies where hierarchy is the rule—in the family, in the social group, and among divine beings. The Kaguru of Tanzania, along with other peoples, believe that such equality is a holy state to be safely achieved by a few divinities alone.

As happens along the Niger River, tribes whose precincts border on one another may entertain radically opposed beliefs concerning twins. One group kills them, the other yokes twins to its own spiritual and material advantage. In South Africa, some Thonga tribes consider them a special defilement, while others openly rejoice at the birth of twins: the women beg the mother for a portion of her body fat with which they smear their own bodies in the hope of conceiving twins. The only correspondences between these mutually exclusive beliefs are their perplexing, uncanny contradictions, and their testament to the symbolic power of twins, whose sacred and profane agencies hold peoples around the world in nearly universal awe.

Similarly, in our own society, there is about the psychology of twin children an aspect of the uncanny. For every feature of child development that we recognize, there seems to be in twins a corresponding exaggeration, attenuation, or inversion, a slight twisting of context, or something unfamiliar eerily grafted onto what we already know. So much more strongly do twins resemble each other than other members of the family that they form a unit apart. They appear to be unrelated to their relatives, as if they were two who had originally been orphaned and then adopted by the family which now feeds and rears them.

In their early rivalry, the ferocity of two who are both so small—who fight in their carriage or declare a wish that the other were dead—may be eerie to behold. At the same time, the cooperation and collaboration between twins constitute an infant altruism unexperienced by single brothers and sisters, whose services to one another are generally much more grudgingly rendered. Yet it is an altruism which the twins do not extend to others, whom they often lock out in the strength of their self-absorption.

Although the relations of twins bear a deeper than surface resemblance to the intimacies of adults, their overdependent bond with one another belies their apparent maturity. The surfeit of satisfactions twins may enjoy with one another may arrest development in the same way as emotional deprivation does in other children.

As an infant, a twin is constantly seeing his own emotions acted out in front of him. When their mother comes into or leaves the room, each twin will want to see or follow her. A new object will excite the curiosity of both, and each will reach to possess it. Something will frighten one twin, and both may want to flee. Food will stimulate a joint hunger, or an unpleasant smell a common disgust. Like a bureaucracy of two, twins will often consult with each other to reach agreement on activities that do not necessarily require the participation of both. Through their joint choreography of experience, twins become adults bound together emotionally by the indestructible visual contract of their absolute identity, by the perfect pitch of their mutual sensitivity, as if each were an exactly replicated voodoo doll of the other.

Twins are a species of the uncanny, of phenomena that lie in the region between the familiar and the unfamiliar, the revealed and the hidden—ambiguous phenomena which provoke apprehension. In a brilliant essay on the subject published in 1919, Freud defined the uncanny as that class of the fearful "which leads back to something long known to us, once very familiar," and now quite forgotten. Freud saw the aspect of fear in the uncanny as extending through the entire continuum of intellectual uncertainty, vague unease, eeriness, fright, dread, horror, and outright terror.

We cannot say that every instance of the fearful is uncanny. To each, some other quality must be added to produce an uncanny experience. That quality is the familiar, the congenial, a certain something which invites us to feel at ease, at the same time that we are aware of an apprehension rising within us. The phenomenon in question seems to be in some way displaced, or at a tangent to the original model for an experience that we cannot now fully describe or recollect. Or something previously hidden suddenly erupts out of what had been a familiar setting, strangely altering its place in our experience.

When we meet a pair of twins, they may stir in us those forgotten moments when, as either adults or children, we imagined a double for ourselves, a twin with perfect empathy. Even if we have never visualized such a figure, we are likely to have felt an ardent wish to encounter such understanding in someone we have yet to meet, or to have rued its absence in those we know. Then, suddenly, in the duplicated person of twins, a representation of what would allay our lament or fulfill our desire appears before us. But because the desire remains buried, or the lament is not quite remembered, we cannot immediately identify what it is that we experience as familiar. The reaction occurs in advance of analysis, the feelings before there are words. The memory traces of this perfectly empathic companion are activated but not identified as we confront an actual pair of twins. And so the associations that ultimately lead back to our phantom double produce in us a feeling of vague unease, as though we had been prematurely separated from someone of great value. We may then experience these twins as an uncanny phenomenon.

Whatever their age, twins suggest the qualities of a married couple of advanced years, of two who possess an immense amount of shared history. To speak with twins is to find oneself in the midst of an elaborate drama of whose previous action we have no knowledge, other than the strange richness that it seems to contribute to the twins' present exchange with us. Like an anthropologist probing a foreign culture, we know twins may have an established language, signals, and sensitivities not found elsewhere. One twin may casually interrupt, and the other graciously accede, knowing his twin will say what he himself had been thinking. Because of these traits, with twins we are unusually alert, and we bring an exceptional energy to our infrequent encounters with them.

Twins occupy a psychic space disproportionate to the physical area occupied by two single persons because of the suggestive power of two identical beings together. Implicit in a pair of identical twins is the binding strength of an alliance, which may be benign or malevolent. Each is able to mask the true identity of the other, or assume his twin's role in life. The possible confusion of one with the other leaves us at an unnatural disadvantage, just that much less competent to order our perceptions. In a small but nevertheless real and uncanny way, the interchangeability of twins gives us a taste of chaos—an anomaly the more unsettling because of the order implicit in any visual duplication.

There is, in fact, a mystery about the biological purpose served by identical twins. Litter mates borne by other mammals are not identical twins. Such multiple births clearly enhance a species' prospects for survival, but the additional advantage gained by exactly duplicated features remains unclear. Identical twinning may perhaps be an evolutionary accident, a mutation whose original purpose is now completely lost to scientific view, but which nevertheless goes on blindly recurring for no discernible reason, like a phonograph needle stuck in a record groove, repeatedly playing the same two beats of music.

In the absence of certain knowledge, the identical nature of twins may momentarily suggest some atavistic scheme in nature in which *Homo sapiens* would have formed a far more hierarchical society. Perhaps we might have become a version of Aldous Huxley's brave new world, ordered by an exact division of labor in which the members of a given functional class, analogous to worker and soldier ants, were all identical twins of one another: standardized men and women in uniform lots, the same voice from a profusion of separate throats, the same image repeated on hundreds, perhaps thousands of faces—a nightmare vision of vast, indistinguishable sameness.

Huxley's anti-utopia was based on the idea of cloning, or the indefinite replication of some chosen human being. The particular repulsion attached to this idea is, of course, that of the standardization of something we reflexively consider unique: the individual personality. For that moment in which twins become the symbol of such genetic and social engineering, a second uncanny repulsion is created in addition to the prospective one of a brave new world of herds of identical twins. It is that the symbol takes over in full the significance of the things symbolized—two individual twins and whatever constitutes their everyday actualities.

Two distinguished biologists, P. B. Medawar and Jacques Monod, once held a formal discussion about genetic engineering. They ended by agreeing that both the dangers and the benign possibilities of gene manipulation had been grossly exaggerated. Monod, however, made an exception for cloning, which he believed was a definite possibility. Although Medawar thought that the conditions necessary for cloning would be extremely difficult to control, the very fact that such a discussion was held is itself unnerving. This sober dialogue between two eminences from the world of biological science eerily collapses the distinction between the imaginary and the real. Human cloning, which before had only been a metaphor in an anti-utopian novel, is suddenly before us as a real possibility. We wonder in what world we shall soon live where any of us could undergo indefinite replication or twinning. Merely contemplating the social and political process necessary to decide who would be fit for cloning is another eerie train of thought. The impending reality supersedes in uncanniness the fictionalized world which initially depicted the process.

In more subtle ways the sight of twins may momentarily stimulate in us animistic habits of thought: those tendencies to conceive of the observable world—human beings, plants, animals or even inanimate objects—as inhabited by the unobservable, by unseen, powerful spirits. Animism, or magical thinking, is not limited to aboriginal peoples. As we watch children at play, observing no distinction between living and inanimate objects, conversing with dolls as though with real human beings, declaring that a fantasy twin "occupies" a chair that appears to be empty, we are reminded of how we too passed through an animistic phase in our psychic development.

Indeed, although we have presumably discarded that way of thinking as adults, most of us still retain vestiges of it. In his essay on the uncanny, Freud connected these animistic traces of thought to uncanny experiences. At some subconscious level of feeling, we do not entirely subscribe to the empiricist's point of view in approaching the world. When something happens in our lives which seems eerily or fearfully to confirm the animism we believe we have surmounted, we get a feeling of the uncanny, even though our rational judgment has already rejected the animistic interpretation.

In those moments when the psychic undercurrent of our response to identical twins supersedes the commonsense reality of their presence, we might begin to wonder whether we have passed beyond the limits of the real into some realm of the fantastic. Something about their identical features suggests all the unerring exactitude of industrial mass production, implying that what we thought was alive might possess only the mechanical animation of automatons, or the limited mobility of puppets, whose movements are governed by some unseen mover behind the curtain. In turn, this association may trigger its converse: that what we have just imagined as only mechanical now appears unmistakably full of life, bringing with it an eerie infusion of vitality. Twins intimate the dual suggestion that what is living might not be alive and that the lifeless might be animate.

Another uncanny nuance of the symbolic power associated with twins is akin to the primitive's fear that a camera and its photographs will rob him of his spiritual essence. In the animistic mind, to duplicate a human being in the form of an image is itself deviltry. Twins hint that they have exercised the same surreptitious power, as if the person whose essence were stolen had conspired in the sorcery, not a victim but a willing agent in the magical grafting of the second self. If two persons now share the resources that had originally belonged to one, there must be a corresponding enervation, a thinning of substance and vitality. Their single sign of intense life might be a kind of soulless radiation, a cynical pleasure at so flamboyantly laying aside the burdens of self-definition.

As we consider the unique closeness of twins, we may shy away from a certain ambiguity about their relations with one another. They are brothers or sisters, yet there are no physical differences between them—only their stark identities protrude. With the same voices and ways of speaking twins belie whatever real personality distinctions each of them actually possesses. We may immediately identify the warmth and understanding of their relationship with aspects of love with which we are familiar, but it seems that there remains a certain unnamable something that binds the two of them more tightly together, some powerful residual affect beyond our own experience of relationship, an emotional bond which does not seem reducible to analytic terms.

This uncertainty over the exact nature of their union feeds on a sexual ambiguity as well. In their less vital moments, twins may suggest the sexlessness of eunuchs, as though their overdependence were a sort of libidinal entropy that left them unconcerned with the pleasures of the body. Conversely, in the presence of twins whose sex is the opposite of ours, we might imagine them as bisexual, as two who are in step with the social convention of heterosexuality, but who always return to the twin for a more intense sexual fusion. Twins whose sex is the same as ours may suggest a homosexuality, a narcissistic tenderness, or an uninhibited sensuality never experienced with the opposite sex.

At the same time as twins suggest these multiple violations of the incest taboo, they call to mind that aspect of the uncanny which arises from something forbidden or disgusting which ought to have been kept hidden, but which has nevertheless come to light. Such associations to twins are both more and less removed from reality than we might suppose. An authoritative study of homosexuality in twins was made by the geneticist Franz J. Kallman. Although the rate of homosexuality among male identical twins is no higher than that among the general population, Kallman found that in 95 percent of the cases where one twin was overtly homosexual, the other twin was homosexual as well—as compared to concordances of 11.5 percent among fraternal twin pairs, and about the same rate among brothers of different ages within the same family. Moreover, in most instances where both twins of a pair were homosexual, the same sexual roles—dominant or submissive, masculine or feminine—were taken by both. Most of the twins studied reported that their homosexual proclivities had developed independently of, and often at a great distance from each other. All categorically denied any history of sexual relations with one another, and disclaimed having any detailed knowledge of their twins' sex life, even though many were living together at the time of the survey.

The incidence of schizophrenia, like that of homosexuality, is no higher among twins than that in the general population (1 percent). But while the rates of concordance, according to Kallman, are 9.2 percent in parents of a schizophrenic twin, 14 percent in a full sibling, and 14 percent in a fraternal twin, the concordance rate among identical twins is 86 percent. Other investigators have confirmed this tendency, although their figures are somewhat lower than Kallman's (66–76 percent). While the data indicate an indisputable genetic predisposition, the environmental influence of one twin on the other may be the more determining variable—for twins who are separated early in life, the concordance rate is much lower. It is also the generally submissive twin who becomes more seriously ill.

There are similar patterns in cases of communicated insanity, clinically known as a *folie à deux*. Frequently taking the form of acute paranoid delusions, it is most common among those living together in extreme seclusion—husband and wife, brother and sister, parent and child, identical twins, or companions of the same sex. The passive partner comes under the psychotic dominance of the other because of the presence in him of the same kind of problems. A *folie à deux* seems to be a form of refuge against what is perceived as a hostile outside world.

One case involved a pair of identical twins in an army hospital ward. In an intricate, continuous mime, each removed his clothes at the same time as the other; one would stand rigidly at attention without having been commanded to do, and so would his twin, for torturous lengths of time. It was impossible to separate the two of them except by force. Once they had been moved to opposite ends of a long corridor, they communicated by means of shrill whistling. A question to one would be answered by both at once. Spot inspections repeatedly showed identical trivia in their pockets. They sometimes switched leadership roles, although one was more often dominant than the other; both thought their bathrobes emanated magical powers, declared that the more passive of the two had been permanently affected by a drug concealed in a poisoned banana, and had frequent auditory hallucinations warning them that they were in danger. Each would both spit on the floor at any disturbance, ignoring all orders to stop the practice.

The concordances among identical twins for homosexuality, schizophrenia, and *folie à deux* are disturbing in part because the phenomena themselves are uncomfortable to contemplate, even though we are at least dimly aware of such tendencies buried in some remote corner of our being, as faint, uneasy traces of our own dissociated selves. Uncannily, when they manifest themselves fully in both halves of a pair of twins, these conditions appear to have been demonically induced, as if one twin were a revenant from the spirit world, come back to carry off his brother for having survived him.

As a less exaggerated metaphor of the inescapable interdependence between identical twins, consider for a moment the plight of Siamese twins attached to one another just below the breast plate, as is not uncommon. There is not one movement of any significance that either is able to perform independently of the other. From the point of view of a single individual, there is an absolute lack of privacy; in public places, there is no escape from curious stares. Always taking care not to rend the symbiotic tissue which keeps both of them alive, each twin must conduct his whole life as a series of minute and major accommodations to the other, so that finally they incorporate their psyches and the two bodies become one person.

The interdependence of identical twins is less visible, but nevertheless acted out by them. One twin is often unable to conceive of himself apart from the other, or to think of the other except in terms of himself. Their uncommon closeness seems triply determined—once by their genetic identity, a second time by the psychic conditioning of the scrutinies pressed upon twins by others, and yet again by the inordinate amount of time twins normally spend together.

One possible result of this multiple determinism is narcissistic dependence, dramatically depicted in Thomas Mann's short story, *The Blood of the Walsungs*. The nineteen-year-old Aarenhold twins, Sigmund and Sieglinde, are alike except for their sex. With a refinement made possible by their father's *arriviste* money, they despise him for his crudeness. At dinner and elsewhere together, their gazes frequently seek each other's, "melting together in an understanding from which everybody else was shut out." Living in regal isolation, each elaborates the accoutrements of life in so rich and varied a fashion that little time is left for life itself. When they speak, it is as though the entire world existed only for their "witty condemnation."

Sieglinde is engaged to be married to a highly placed civil servant, whom she ridicules behind his back for his earnestness, his naive curiosity, his desire to please. Flaunting her closeness to her twin brother, she refuses to permit her fiance to go with the two of them to the opera, where the Wagnerian *Ring* cycle is being performed. There, they sit holding hands. Although critical of the performance, the twins are brought to the realization that passion—which they normally mock as a "blunder"—begets creation and real life, which in turn shapes further passion.

They return home, engulfed by a half-acknowledged despair over the superfluity of their lives. Sigmund goes to his room, where he sits contemplating his reflection in a triple mirror. Sieglinde enters, and he examines her in exactly the same way. "You are just like me," he says. "Everything about you is just like me." Defying the taboo against incest, they begin to caress one another.

> They loved each other with all the sweetness of the senses, each for the other's costly well-being and delicious fragrance. They breathed it in, this fragrance, with its languid and voluptuous abandon, like self-centered invalids, consoling themselves for the loss of hope.

They love each other "for their own rare uselessness," and indulge a final consumption of the self.

Mann's story is an uncanny parable because it unmasks the insulated world of the twins behind their layered sophistication, their condescension to all experience. Mann's elegant language, and his surgical, ruthless skill in exposing the repellent nature of the twins' self-absorption, cast eerie effects. Although it is not essentially about the nature of twins, Mann's story nevertheless uncannily suggests the experience of many narcissistically dependent twins, whose androgynous character hints at forbidden intimacies.

Thornton Wilder, the novelist and playwright, was himself a twin. His novel, *The Bridge of San Luis Rey,* set in late nineteenth century Peru, includes an orphaned pair of twins. Their names, Manuel and Esteban, "were not as useful to them as our names are to most of us, for no one ever succeeded in telling the boys apart." They had their own secret language, but resorted to it only when they were alone together or "at great intervals in moments of stress whispered it in the presence of others."

Their identical appearance was the object of so many jokes and comments that, ashamed, they made a tacit agreement not to appear together in public. Yet along with their shame, they felt a need for each other so intense as to seem terrible, dark, even forbidden. Earning their living as scribes, they always worked together, and toward others they remained silent and unapproachable. For Manuel and Esteban, "all the world was remote and strange and hostile except one's brother."

But then Manuel fell in love with a beautiful woman, an actress, who was also the Viceroy's mistress. Esteban, observing the growth of his brother's passion, discovered that the meaning had gone out of his life. Watching Manuel and the actress together one night, Esteban felt himself "shrink away into space, infinitely tiny, infinitely unwanted. He took one more glance at the tableau of love painted on his brother's countenance, at all the paradise from which he was shut out, and turned his face to the wall."

Feeling guilty and disloyal at his own despair, he said, "Go and follow her, Manuel. Don't stay here. You'll be happy. There's room for all of us in the world." Aware of the pain his brother was suffering, Manuel suddenly pictured

> Esteban going a long way off and saying good-bye many times as he went. He was filled with terror: by the light of it he saw that all the other attachments in the world were shadows, or the illusions of fever. . . . In his excitement he groped for a means of holding his brother who seemed to be receding into the distance. And at once, in one unhesitating stroke of the will, he removed the actress from his heart.

One night, Manuel fell and tore open the flesh on his knee. Infection and fever set in. Crazed with pain and rage, Manuel cried out to his brother: "God condemn your soul to the hottest hell there is. A thousand devils torture you forever, Esteban. For coming between me and what was mine by right." At dawn, Manuel had no memory of the things he had said. But the attacks of pain recurred, and on the third night he died. Esteban left the apartment and refused to go back to it. Asked which twin he was, he answered, "Manuel." For weeks he wandered despondently through the streets. Finally one day he tried to hang himself. Surprised in the act by his employer, he fell to the floor, crying out, "I am alone, alone, alone."

Esteban's shock comes with a tortured immobility of the self, a self on the dawning edge of the wholly unbidden knowledge that he had existed as almost nothing more than a series of reactions to the union formed with this other person. For a moment, the pathos of Esteban's cry seems to snap the spell of the uncanny, whose aura surrounded the twins to the degree of their overdependence, to the extent that Manuel was able to proclaim his desires for the actress and his fury at Esteban only in a fevered delirium. But even his experience of his brother's death resonates with the eerie. When Manuel was alive, it was the world which was strange and distantly hostile. Now it is himself which Esteban experiences as unutterably alien, suddenly uncoupled from those extraordinary sympathies of which he had hardly been conscious before. His is the pain and horror of a symbiosis sundered.

||| Of all emotional attachments, that between twins seems the least able to accommodate separation and death. Many twins can picture themselves surviving the death of their husbands or wives or children, but they are frequently unable to imagine living without their twin. Whether married or single, with or without children, each pair of twins is the last of a given species. There is no way to duplicate the resemblance they already so perfectly share, no way in which to pass it on intact to the next generation. Death has an

additional finality for twins that it possesses for no one else. As with Esteban, it will often leave the surviving twin in an egoless vacuum of the self, a black hole of grief beyond the sorrow which death more usually occasions, as if one had stepped in front of a mirror and saw no affirming reflection.

Jonathan McCullogh, an identical twin and a highly successful businessman now in his forties, had enjoyed his twinship immensely as a child. "I was never lonely," he says. "My brother was a treasurehold of child's pleasures." His mother found it difficult to tell them apart, but took great pride in them, and often referred to them simply as "the twins." So complete was their sharing of experience that it was later difficult for Jonathan to recall whether certain events happened to him or to his brother.

Around the age of five or six, however, Jonathan began having a recurrent nightmare: he would hear an intruder banging on the door or see a figure entering the room with a knife, and would observe that James's bed was unoccupied. At the same time as the nightmares, Jonathan developed an intense fear of going into the cellar, either alone or with his twin—although in the presence of someone other than James the anxiety would be relieved.

At college, where both were superior students, the twins followed the same course of studies. As is not uncommon with identical twins, Jonathan secretly pictured James as a trifle taller, a bit more handsome, and certainly brighter—even though no more than a small fraction of a percentage point separated their grades. During his second year, Jonathan refused to talk to James about money or about his sex life, both of which he spent totally apart from his twin. At the end of the spring semester Jonathan and James were to take final examinations. Just before one exam, James had mentioned an abdominal pain. But when Jonathan saw his brother leave the room, before he himself was halfway through the examination, he supposed that James had simply given his usually excellent performance. Determined not to be surpassed, Jonathan stayed until the end of the allotted time, thoroughly going through what he had written.

Afterward, Jonathan learned from the police what had happened: James had collapsed in a subway station and been taken to a hospital, where his illness has been diagnosed as appendicitis. Inexplicably, no surgery was performed until several days later, when James had already developed peritonitis. With his brother in delirium, Jonathan repeatedly assured him that he, James, had received an "A" on his examination. On the following day James died while Jonathan was at a movie.

Jonathan's initial response was a massive denial of his brother's death.

> I refused to look at the corpse and I didn't even go into the funeral parlor. When the coffin was lowered into the grave, I averted my eyes. Afterwards, whenever I met anyone who didn't know my brother had died, I didn't inform him. When asked, "How is your brother?" I'd reply, "He's all right."

> Every evening for some time after James' death, I would say "Good night" to his empty bed. When I took walks by myself, I'd talk with him, asking his opinion about various plans of mine.

Jonathan would also converse with James on visits to the grave, and was often convinced that he heard a response in the rush of wind through the trees or in the far-away call of a bird. He had appropriated James's club cap in exchange for his own, in which he had James buried. He also began to use a J., for his brother's first name, as his own middle initial. He asked friends to write memoirs of James, which he then stored in a shoebox along with other mementoes. "For years," he says, "it was my most valuable possession."

Ten years after James died, an uncle died in Jonathan's arms on the way to a hospital, during a severe attack of asthma. The event triggered a nightmare in which Jonathan saw his mirror image leave his body and slowly float like a phantom toward the ceiling. He would try desperately to pull the image back to himself, only to have its matterless form slip through his fingers and rise once again. He awakened in a cold sweat, feeling intense anxiety at finding himself alone. Traveling home from work on the subway the next day, he felt acutely claustrophobic, and was suddenly doubled over with abdominal pains. The death of Jonathan's uncle had reactivated the trauma of James's death a decade earlier. His nightmare was the enactment of his efforts to deny to his emotions the irreversible fact that his brother was dead. The claustrophobia and abdominal pains were psychosomatic reminders of an event Jonathan had tried to eradicate from his memory. He now decided to seek professional help.

While most people in psychoanalysis will transfer onto their therapist the fear, anger, love and guilt they associate with their parents, Jonathan in effect converted the therapist into his twin. "I had already tried," he says, "to re-create my relationship with James with several friends and two women I had almost married." But his period in therapy was particularly fertile ground for the acting out of this tendency. Like twins emotionally locked out from everyone else, here are two people, patient and analyst, who share a common room closed off from the rest of the world, and whose intensely common purposes are focused through an intimacy unlike any other, one which is often expressed in a secret language—that of therapy argot.

At the beginning, Jonathan continued in effect to deny his brother's death. He could accept the therapist's suggestions only after repeating them in his own voice—a process that either unconsciously transferred the source of the suggestions to his twin brother James, or implied that his brother, still alive in Jonathan's psyche, approved them. There were moments when the therapist's room became for Jonathan the dark, claustrophobic cellar of his childhood home. The presence of the therapist did not always assuage these fears, and sometimes even intensified them. There were other times when Jonathan experienced in the room and the company of the therapist all the comfort, reassurance and tender happiness of being with his twin.

Jonathan's urge to find a twin became clear in his attachment to the Landers, another pair of identical twins with whom for a while he spent much of his time. Living out a fantasy that is experienced by many identical twins, the Landers, Jonathan says, had "married two identical twin women, and each couple has identical twin children. Everything is one for these couples, including their bank account; all live together perfectly happy." Jonathan had sometimes fantasized an accidental exchange of wives, the mixup culminating in a blissful androgyny. And he now began to elaborate a fantasy of living in a house near the therapist.

Slowly, Jonathan began to face long-buried feelings of deprivation. He imagined having been born as an only child, remembering for the first time in years his secret childhood envy of friends who were single children, and created retrospective fantasies of being alone in his mother's womb, a solitary life luxuriating in undisturbed satiety.

He went back over the nightmare of his childhood. As a child he had assumed that the intruder into the room was his brother; now, reversing the interpretation, Jonathan recognized himself as the intruder—banging on the door, threatening violence, determined to secure a place for himself.

He realized that he had identified himself as the unwanted intruder because James was older, though only by the minutes required for a second delivery. His family had been poor, there often had not been enough food for everyone, and these privations became repeated occasions for feeling the guilt of an intruder. Jonathan, the second-born, existed by sufferance alone, haunted by a sense of guilt that colored his whole personality and behavior. Playing both the agent and the victim of the violence in the dream helped Jonathan to understand how he had taken his brother into himself, incorporating his twin into his own system of psychic checks and balances. He metaphorized this internalized twin as a kind of dybbuk—the spirit of someone dead, which takes possession of a living body and makes itself manifest through the suffering it causes its corporeal host. With one of the self-destructive inversions at which the psyche is so adroit, Jonathan had converted his earlier instinctive wish to be a single individual into a punishment inflicted on him by a conscience that had the internalized twin at the controls. So long as he suffered in this way, he could go on denying his brother's death. To admit fully that his brother was dead was unconsciously equated in Jonathan's mind with killing him, with becoming the murderous intruder.

Another twin, Eric Davidson, a writer of history textbooks, had a nightmare of his own. He too pictured himself as the unwanted intruder, and was consistently more submissive than his brother Sam, whom he viewed as superior to him in athletic and scholastic abilities. When Eric was twenty, a friend sketched for him Victor Hugo's story of "The Man in the Iron Mask," the imaginary twin brother of Louis XIV of France. In the story, out of fear that as adults Louis and his twin, Philippe, would quarrel over the succession to the throne, Philippe had been secluded since infancy, first in a remote country house and later in a solitary cell in the Bastille.

Several nights after hearing this story, Eric had a nightmare of being trapped in a dungeon, his elbows and knees enclosed in metal braces, his head covered by a metal helmet with a grilled visor. "I slowly became haunted," says Eric, "by the sense that Sam had something to do with my horrifying predicament, but I couldn't say what or how." With the residual disbelief that still lingers in the psyche gripped by a nightmare, Eric heard himself insisting, "It is nothing but a dream. It is time to awaken from it." But then—still as part of the nightmare—"I realized that what I was experiencing was real after all." With a new wave of fear the feeling that he was about to wake up was repeated. Unable to distinguish dreaming from being awake, Eric began to entertain the possibility that he "might already be dead."

Later Eric read the Victor Hugo story for himself. He experienced a particular resonance in the bitter realization of Philippe, the Iron Mask, that he is fatally condemned not to know who he is: "Am I a man, have I a name? I alone can say yes. Well, then, I say no." The Iron Mask's one real act of self-definition is the single power to see himself as possessing a mutilated identity: "I am a living corpse conscious of itself, alive within its coffin." Through the frightening auspices of his nightmare, Eric realized "how I had seen myself totally in terms of Sam. The awareness gave me a freedom from Sam which I increasingly felt I needed."

Like Jonathan McCullogh, Eric felt that he was "changing from an identical twin into a non-identical one." It is doubtful whether identical twins ever attain the status of ordinary brothers and sisters, since in both affirmative and negative ways they share so much. But Jonathan's observation nevertheless describes the process of emotional dissociation most twins must undergo if they are to avoid the crippling effects of overidentification with one another, a process no less necessary than breaking the bond of dependency on one's parents.

Jonathan's efforts to deny that James was dead reveal another uncanny aspect of being a twin, one that is present in Eric's dream as well. Many elements of Jonathan's psychic history—his suppressed desire to be alone, the childhood nightmare of the intruder, the fears of the cellar, the trauma of his uncle's death, and his repeated desires to fuse with some image of the twin—recur over and over.

What is uncanny here is precisely the recurrence of these situations, feelings, and events, the involuntary return to the function they have in constricting any genuine sense of an individual self. It is as though one were lost in the medieval quarter of some European city, trying to find one's way along winding and narrow streets, only to end again and again, as if by fate, in the same small, dismal plaza. Psychically, twins seem fated always to be tied to one another, to a degree and for reasons that may for long, as in Jonathan's case, remain unsuspected.

Unless we are totally hardened against superstition or animistic habits of thought, we may be tempted to ascribe uncanny meanings to all such obstinate recurrences. Even the process of psychoanalysis may become uncanny in such a context, a shamanistic exploration of the demonic forces in the psyche, which are accessible only through the realms of fantasy and dreams. In the cellar and the dungeon that are Jonathan's and Eric's respective nightmares, there are also silence, darkness, and solitude, all of them very suggestive states for the reactivation of an infantile, morbid anxiety, from which few of us are ever completely free. Out of this anxiety issue all the imagined terrors, the radical uncertainties, and even those sensations Eric experienced at the end of his dream, of being buried, of watching oneself as a kind of living corpse.

IV

The reverse of this morbid state of mind is the twin-hero romance. Underlying it, from the Dioscuri and the Asvins to Superman and the fantasy twins of single or lonely children, is the same fundamental invention of the psyche, the doubling of the self. So we see Castor becoming immortal through the intervention of Pollux, the doubling of the self as insurance against destruction, which is also seen in the practice of the ancient Egyptians, among others, of making twin images of the dead—not only of kings, but also of their servants, cats, dogs, cows, hawks, and other sacred animals. Indeed, as Otto Rank has stressed, the idea of the immortal soul is likewise an immaterial doubling of the self, "an energetic denial of the power of death."

Among many aboriginal peoples, twins, as doubles of one another, often prolong and extend life through the special powers ascribed to them; for each other and for their communities, they are a link between mortality and a spirit or immortal world. When once mythological and animistic habits of thought fall victim to an empirical view of reality, the psychic phenomenon of the doubling of the self does not disappear; instead, it radically alters its character, taking on a new set of conditions which are also vividly and uncannily evoked by actual identical twins.

As we look at twins, we may find ourselves haunted by a sensation that has in some way to do with the eyes, with the act of watching. Eyes are the centerpiece to the exposed and naked face. Set within an extremely narrow field of movement, eyes are nevertheless the most animated organs of the body, ceaselessly registering whatever passes before them. It is the presence of two identical sets of observing eyes—their color and hue, the play of reflections on their glossy surface, their recessed setting in the background of eyebrows, forehead, cheekbones, and upper nose—which may hold our fascinated attention.

If we could give words and analysis to our feelings at that instant, we might see that these twins have suddenly become for us a visual representation of our own acts of self-observation, that ability to be simultaneously both the agent and the audience of our actions. In the duality of their union, twins may embody the Socratic dialogues which occur within each of us, dialogues of a self which questions and a self which answers. Twins personify the fundamental process of individual consciousness: one twin becomes the self that watches the self which acts, the other twin the acting self that is being observed.

The most profound and elusive acts of self-observation are our dreams and fantasies. Their mood is often surreal, suffused by uncanny dissociations which are in reality the most acute dramatizations of our own power to explore who we are. The will to penetrate their mysteries often comes accompanied by eerie trepidations at the impending discovery or rediscovery of buried parts of the self. In this context, twins might then appear to embody the same kind of dream-like enigma which we often seem to be to ourselves. The visual congruence of twins—so perfect that it at once becomes incongruous—casts upon us the same ethereal mood which informs our fantasy life. Twins seem in fact to be surreal disfigurations, strange identical dream figures who appear before us as if in the half-light of the unreal, messengers from out of the unconscious bearing us some needed, even dreaded knowledge of ourselves.

As representations of the self within the self, twins may also evoke our own ability to criticize ourselves. Indeed, the self-critical double within each of us often seems to deliver its judgments in an audible voice, to possess all the formidable reality of another independent person, one who yet remains invisible, an identical but mysterious other being locked inside ourselves. Similarly, twins may metaphorize our own relation to our conscience. One twin becomes the superordinate self which guides the other self through the region of moral and ethical quandaries.

These different aspects of the double within us help explain the power of those great fictions of the double written during the nineteenth century. In most of them, the self within the self is exteriorized by the author as another identical person. Thus, in Edgar Allan Poe's *William Wilson,* no authority has ever been able to curb Wilson's excesses or check his imperious nature—until as a student he is confronted by a rival with the same name who precisely imitates Wilson's own dress, gait, and general manner, and whose single purpose is to yield to Wilson in nothing.

The rival seems to have no weakness that

Wilson might seize to his own advantage. On the contrary, Wilson is constantly aware of his rival's natural dignity and of an occasional, quite inexplicable show of affection toward himself. Infuriatingly, Wilson sees his own affairs become more and more confused with those of his rival; at the same time, it becomes difficult for Wilson to set aside a suspicion of having known the rival somewhere a long time ago.

With each new episode, his rival appears, announces his name, and momentarily shocks Wilson into moral sobriety. As the rival continues to expose his debauchery, Wilson flees from one European capital to another. Unable to bear this enslavement to fear any longer, Wilson turns on his rival and stabs him. Dying, the rival declares: "You have conquered, and I yield. Yet, henceforward art thou also dead—dead to the World, to Heaven, and to Hope! In me didst thou exist—and in my death, see by this image, which is thine own, how utterly thou hast murdered thyself."

In Oscar Wilde's *The Picture of Dorian Gray,* the central figure strikes a devil's bargain: Gray, a modern Narcissus, is to remain young and handsome as the years pass, while his portrait alone records the processes of aging and decay. His life becomes a fastidious sampling of pleasurable sensations, including the pleasure of corrupting others. All the while, even his smallest depravities are registered by his twin in the portrait, as if it had been periodically retouched by unseen brushwork. The portrait gradually becomes the face of a vastly decayed man, all the more repellent for retaining certain lingering traces of its original lustre and perfection. Its visible degeneration strangely grants the portrait-twin a kind of majesterial strength, a stoic bearing up to the ravages of time. Through the withered features of his face there shines an eerie satisfaction. Each time Dorian Gray looks at it, his panic and demoralization increase, until, like William Wilson, he stabs his double—thereby killing himself and restoring to the painting its flawless former beauty.

The theme of the double or twin also occurs in the fiction of Fydor Dostoevsky, E.T.A. Hoffman, Heinrich Von Kleist, Nathaniel Hawthorne, and many others. Unlike the ancient myths of twins as figures in vast cosmological dramas, the fictional purpose of such stories is to dramatize a wholly interior landscape. The frequent inseparability of real twins, the profound effect they have on each other's lives, their strange, mutual attraction even in antipathy—all these qualities have found their way into uncanny tales of the double. Once an assurance of everlasting life, twins have passed into modern literature as allegorical intimations of mortality and moral degeneration.

Other aspects of the double within us appear in fiction, for which twin figures are also used. Imagine, for example, identical twins who cut and comb their hair differently, whose dress is totally dissimilar, who hold unrelated jobs, move in different social worlds, and give every evidence of having lived their lives independently. Encountering the two of them at once, we observe these disparities with a momentary subliminal shock. The twins appear unnatural in this light because we are not accustomed to pairing so much diversity with so much identity. At some level, the twins seem less to be twins than alternative selves, materialized alter egos.

In the mood of Henry James's *The Jolly Corner,* these highly differentiated twins may jostle buried associations to the selves we might have become, to those feasible options which once formed part of our spectrum of choices about what we could do with our lives. We may even have followed the careers of certain people who made the choice that we did not, as if we could track our alternative selves in a dimension parallel to our own. Curious to see what it made of these people, we might have experienced the ache of what that choice could have made of us—of whether this alternative self might have had a larger life than our own. Like James's Spencer Brydon, we may yearn in fantasy to meet this double of ours, this identical twin of our unchosen possibilities.

Highly distinctive twins may prompt us to speculate about how the steps toward differentiation were taken by them: each could not have failed to realize that practically anything done by his twin was also something he himself could have undertaken. Incrementally, the differences between them widened and increased in number until, at some point, each twin experienced the shock of recognizing the irreversible: in high definition, they had developed into distinct personalities who no longer were able to become the self realized by the other twin.

As with these twins, so with the inevitably increasing distance between the ideal self we might have been and the person we have actually become. We all experience the pain of recognizing the self that hoped for more than has been attained. Highly individualized twins may resurrect in us those strivings of our ambition which adverse circumstances have irretrievably blunted, those oceanic feelings of possibility with which we formerly nourished the illusion of more elastic potentialities. Like twins who cannot escape their identity with one another, we are to some degree tied to this less presentable version of ourselves. In such a mood, twins may legitimize a kind of nostalgia, a soft-focus blend of regret and desire. In some region of our being, like aboriginal peoples who hold to their animistic beliefs, we still cling to a hope of magically achieving our former aspirations.

Conversely, highly individual twins may suggest a deeper integration and acceptance of the self. They might stand in the same relation to one another as Joseph Conrad's secret sharers, each being the one who has guided the other into a region of greater risk and larger responsibility. Each to the other is an autonomous stow-away self, an apprentice to boundary situations, to circumstances of moral ambiguity outside those anticipated by institutional sanctions. This second self, this outlaw twin to our own insecurities, is more determined, less in doubt than the self who lives in fear of responsibility. In recognizing this radical self within, there is a release that transforms the anxiety of risk into an exhilaration, and a necessary surrender to the process of seeing how close the self can come to its own ideal conception.

Like each of us in relation to the best parts of ourselves, Conrad's secret sharers put each other on a constant emotional and moral alert, heighten each other's awareness of being alive, their appreciation of life's miracle in an environment which is basically hostile. They are diarists to one another, chroniclers of the self whose narrative line is a dramatic intimacy, a sharing of their self-doubts and self-experiments, their rehearsal of decisions. They use each other to thicken experience, to shore up the ephemeral and make it yield some more lasting resonance. Theirs is a supportive union that adds meaning and value to the drama of their lives outside it.

Highly individual twins embody all the possible roles in the dialectic of the self; they metaphorize the dramatic dialogues of different aspects of ourselves in counterpoise to others. In contrast, overly dependent twins suggest an inert coexistence, hint that any significant differences which might have emerged between them have been smothered by a kind of willed sameness arising out of fear. This sameness is served by a profound ambivalence which they exhibit toward one another, an ambivalence which all twins experience at some level of intensity beyond what we usually associate with single brothers and sisters. The iron mask of the twin is a congealed rage, a frozen desire to distinguish the self from he or she who so resembles it, a forbidding sense of impotence at attempting such a task, and a consequently arrested sense of self, whether experienced temporarily or in more permanent ways.

Uncannily, this ambivalence answers to a sounding in ourselves. We all established our autonomy through opposition to the received wisdom and experience of crucial figures of authority—fathers, mothers, and all those who subsequently came to resemble them. Like the inescapable fears which real twins have in relation to one another, we felt that these figures of authority would abort, steal or muffle our identities, subordinating what was most unique about us to what was most powerful and unyielding in them. Yet these same figures gave us whatever characteristics allowed us to imagine our rebellion from them originally. Our incorporation of their qualities into ourselves gave us an identical inward resemblance to them; we became psychically twinned to them. Wishing to contest their hold on who we would become, we simultaneously became afraid to strike out against those whom we so much resembled, as if we would lose all sense of who we were. We then experienced these oedipal figures as mutilating twins who inhibited the growth of our individuality.

Similarly, twins may remind us of the ambivalence we feel in our rivalries with our own brothers and sisters, those second selves of ours who also possess lives of their own. We may even feel the ambivalence in more intense ways because the rival brother or sister bears a greater resemblance to us, as well as an evocative resemblance to our parents. They are closer to us in time, compete with us for the same limited family resources. In some or many ways, these rival twins threaten to become better, more dramatically realized versions of ourselves, a threat we also came to feel in relation to peers in the larger world outside the family.

The qualities of the uncanny which attach themselves to twins are as old as human beings on earth. The power of their visual resonance contrasts strongly with the rarity of our encounters with twins. Yet the source of their uncanniness is not their infrequent appearance in our lives; rather, it stems from the subtle, intimate links which exist between the image of twins and certain fundamental conflicts and feelings deeply rooted in our own psyches.

The uncanny impressions twins make on us constitute the reality of moments only. They are the fleeting scenarios and moods which twins are apt to summon forth from us in response to the enormous suggestive power of their identities. These sensations do not always correspond to the reality of twins themselves, although there is more often congruence than not. They do, however, define the reality of our responses to twins. Twins set in motion for us a kaleidoscope of sensations whose evanescence stands in striking contrast to their sheer prolific number, as though twins themselves had conspired to divert us through a maze of conflicting impressions in order to confuse us further about what they really represent.

Our responses to looking at twins are described by the powers of the magical twins dreamed of by the medieval theologian Albertus Magnus: in one twin, the evil on his right side unlocked all bolted doors to his right, while the virtue in his twin's left side closed all *open* doors. Twins unleash a flood of associations, each of which triggers its converse: divine and demonic, superhuman and subhuman, immortal and mortal, sexed and sexless. They are a mixture of the familiar and the unfamiliar, the hidden and the revealed.

Similarly, in looking at twins, we may simultaneously wish to avert our eyes and to stare—to watch, unwilling yet enthralled, as if a curtain were about to go up on something we wanted to keep concealed. Stirring both pathos and wonder, twins seem to float in some mysterious region between resemblance and reality, confounding in their flesh the conventional distinctions between self and other, separation and union, the fantastic and the real. Twins induce a vertigo of the self: they are indisputably two, inescapably one, both and neither at once.

Like the classic Rorschach inkblot, twins mingle the symmetrical and highly ordered with the ambiguous and indeterminate. As with the inkblot, we initially respond with an intellectual and emotional uncertainty. We feel twins have something to tell us about ourselves, that they somehow raise significant questions about all beings, but we cannot quite articulate either the questions or the answers. Quickly, however, we begin to project our own associations onto the anomalous form in front of us. With each projection, we reveal as much about ourselves as we do about what is being observed.

As we respond, for instance, to what appears to be the idyllic closeness of twins, we might wonder whether we desire or expect other people in our lives to be exactly like us—identical twins of the psyche—or if we rigidly exclude those who are fundamentally different. We may discover in ourselves an excessive wish to be dependent, to seclude ourselves in the safety of an undivided, embryonic unity. We may recognize in our revulsion at the inseparability and identity of twins a compulsion to be wholly self-sufficient, or a fear that our own uniqueness will go unrecognized. Twins summon up projections of our own self-disgust, our unnamable fears and inadmissible needs. They play upon our basic insecurities about the limits of our own egos, our condition as more than animals, the tenuous hold we have on our sovereign selves.

As the authors of the great fictions of the double knew perfectly well, twins unwittingly release us into the landscapes of our own unconscious. Twins figure forth all the different aspects of the second self within each of us: the neutral self-observer, the critic of the self, the pursuing and punishing conscience, the self as a vision of horror, the alternative self, the self as secret sharer, the ambivalent self faced with an act of self-definition. Suffused by an aura of the uncanny, our second selves, like twins, seem to emerge from a different order of reality, to possess secrets which our foreground selves are only just beginning to fathom. If our knowledge of these parts of us seems only fragmentary and inferential, it is because the second self is the stranger, is the self overlooked and unrealized, excluded from everyday preoccupations, a shadow self both different from and identified with us.

In contemplating our responses to twins, we may bore through our resistance to seeing the them–in–us. We may become a third brother or sister closing the triangle of our fascination with them, reaching across the uncanny divide which they have learned separates themselves from others. In that moment, the two of them may seize us in a compelling gaze which returns our own fascinated stares. There passes between them and us a mute understanding, as though they were saying in unison: "Do not pull back from what is before you. See by our image, which is your own, how completely we are a part of you." It is then that we become imaginatively twinned to them, and to our own second selves, for twins intensify and make paradigmatic the ancient and universal fears, needs and conflicts which drive us all.

PARALLELS
Photographs by Harvey Stein

"Identical twins are products of a single sperm and a single egg. At an early stage the embryo divides, and the halves eventually become separate individuals. Because the twins carry the same chromosomes and genes, they are always either "look-alike" boys or "look-alike" girls. Non-identical twins are products of two different eggs, fertilized by different individuals, and carry different combinations of chromosomes and genes. Apart from being born together, non-identical (fraternal) twins are no more alike than any two children born separately in a family, and thus may or may not be of the same sex.

ERRATUM

Page 46, line 5, should read: fertilized by two different sperm. They eventually develop into two different individuals, and carry different combinations of chromosomes

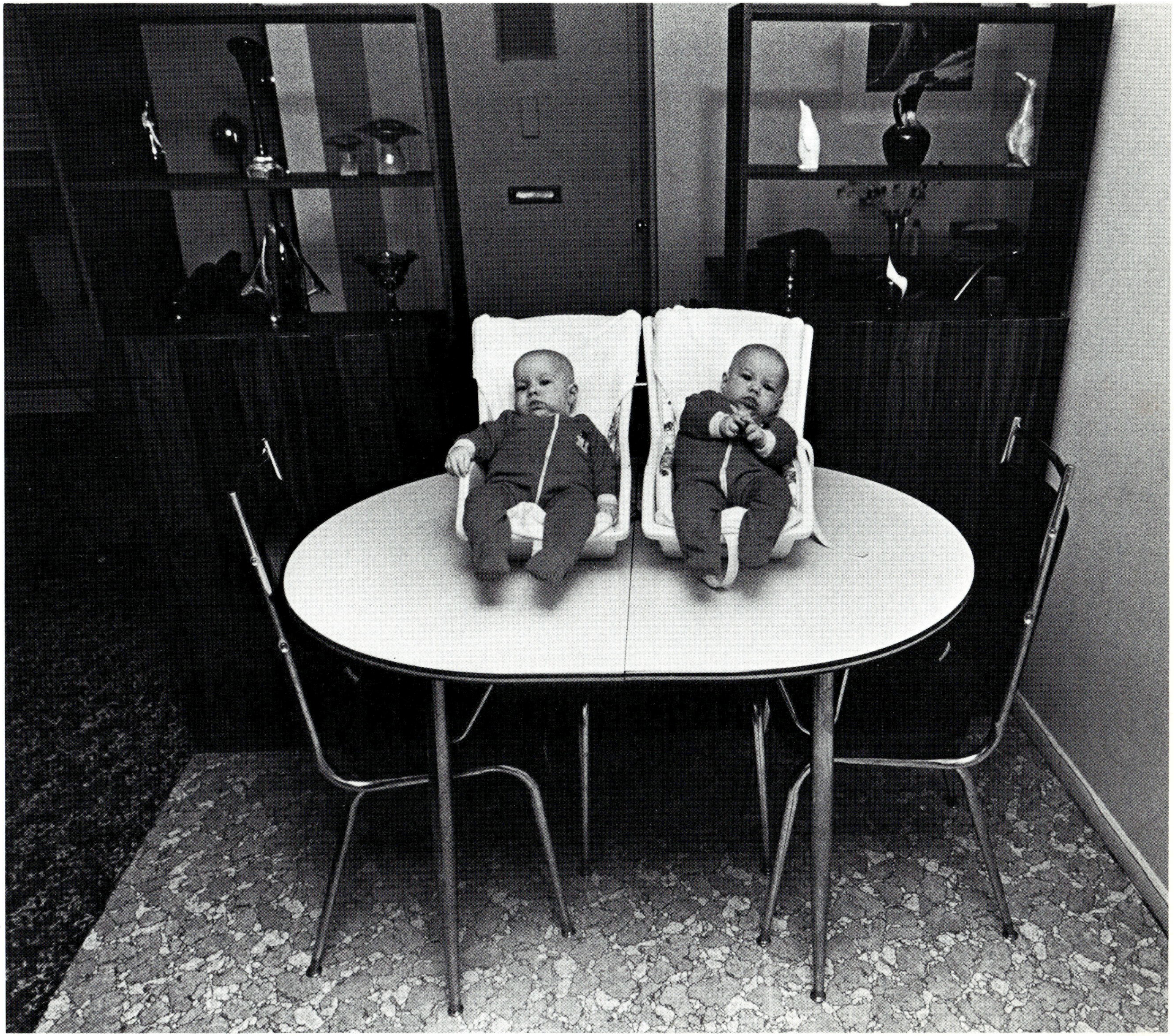

Parents of Infant Twins:
"We feel it is a privilege to have twins. Indeed, it is something special. Not that we did anything special or that we felt a certain extra virility. No, it is special as an act of God. We just carried out His will. And we are very pleased."

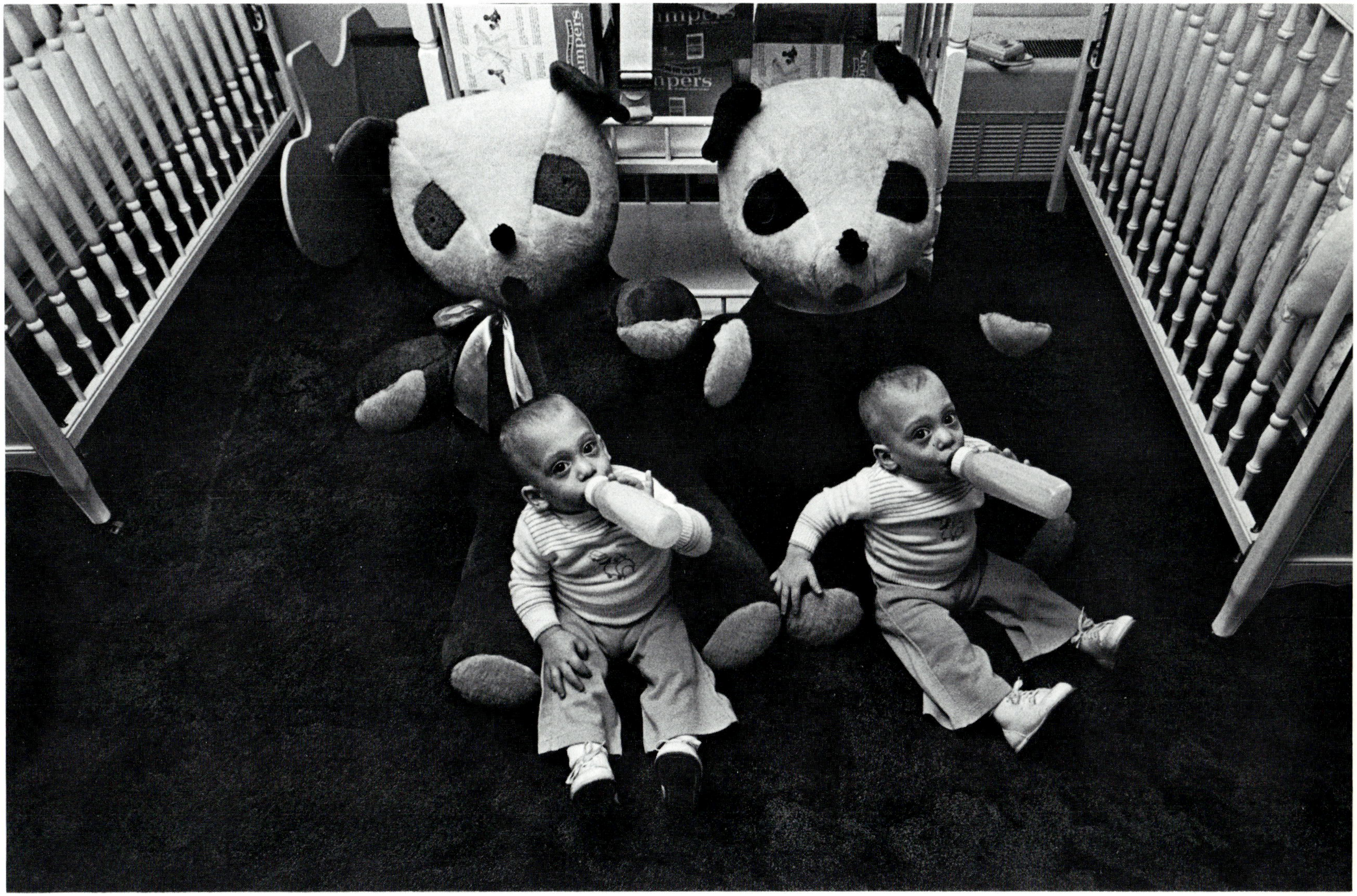

Mother of Young Twins:
"Every time I'm out with the twins, I'm approached by strangers who say the dumbest things. 'Too bad you didn't have a boy and a girl.' Or 'maybe next time you'll have boys.' People are very curious—it's as if they'd never seen twins before. It's gotten to the point that I dread going outside with the twins."

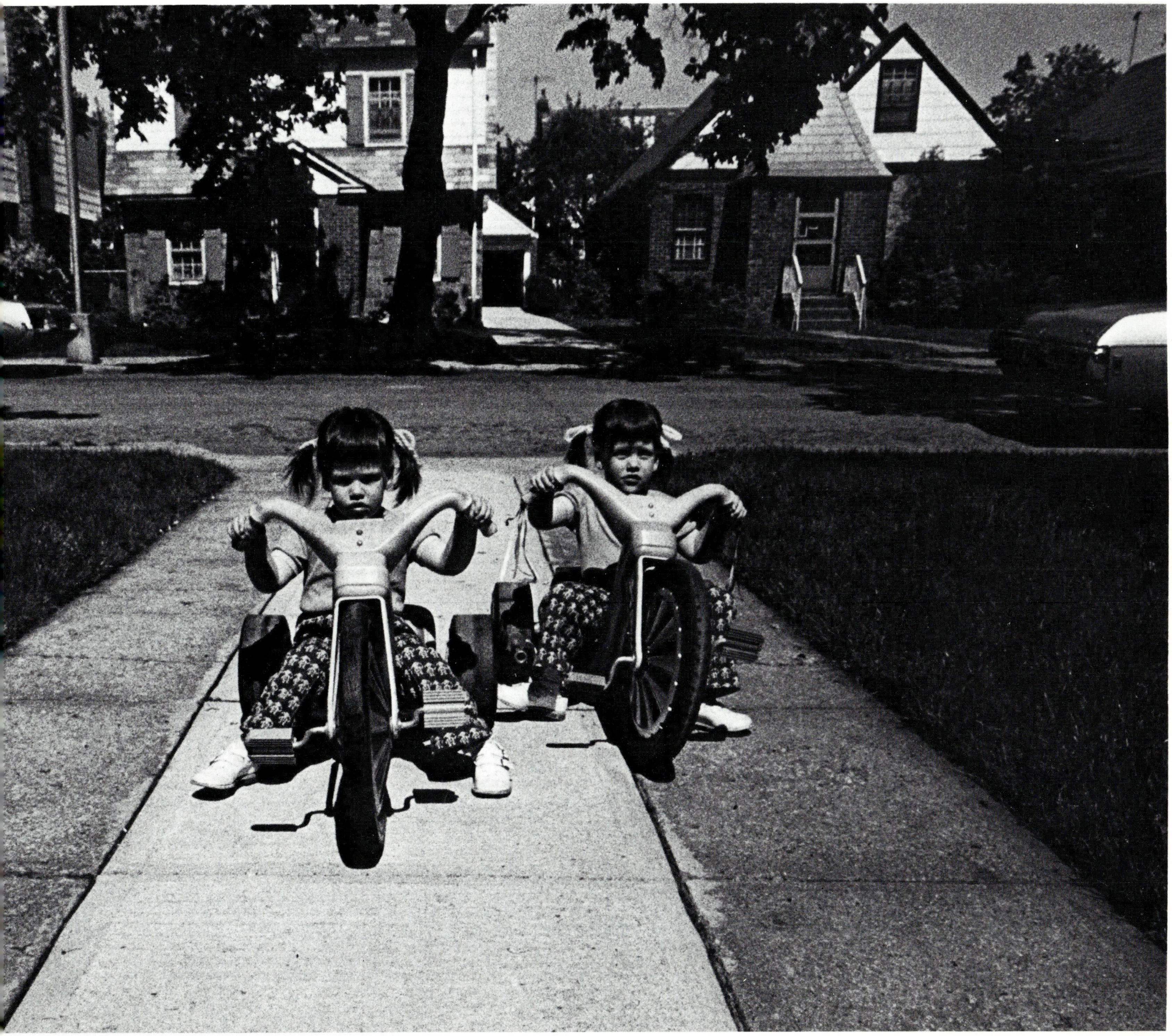

"The earliest memories of myself include my twin. During my childhood, I can't remember anything of my life where my twin was not part of it."

"Sometimes we enjoy tricking people by answering for each other. When we do this, even for a short while, I usually forget who I really am and think I'm my twin."

"I talk to my twin just as if I'm talking to myself."

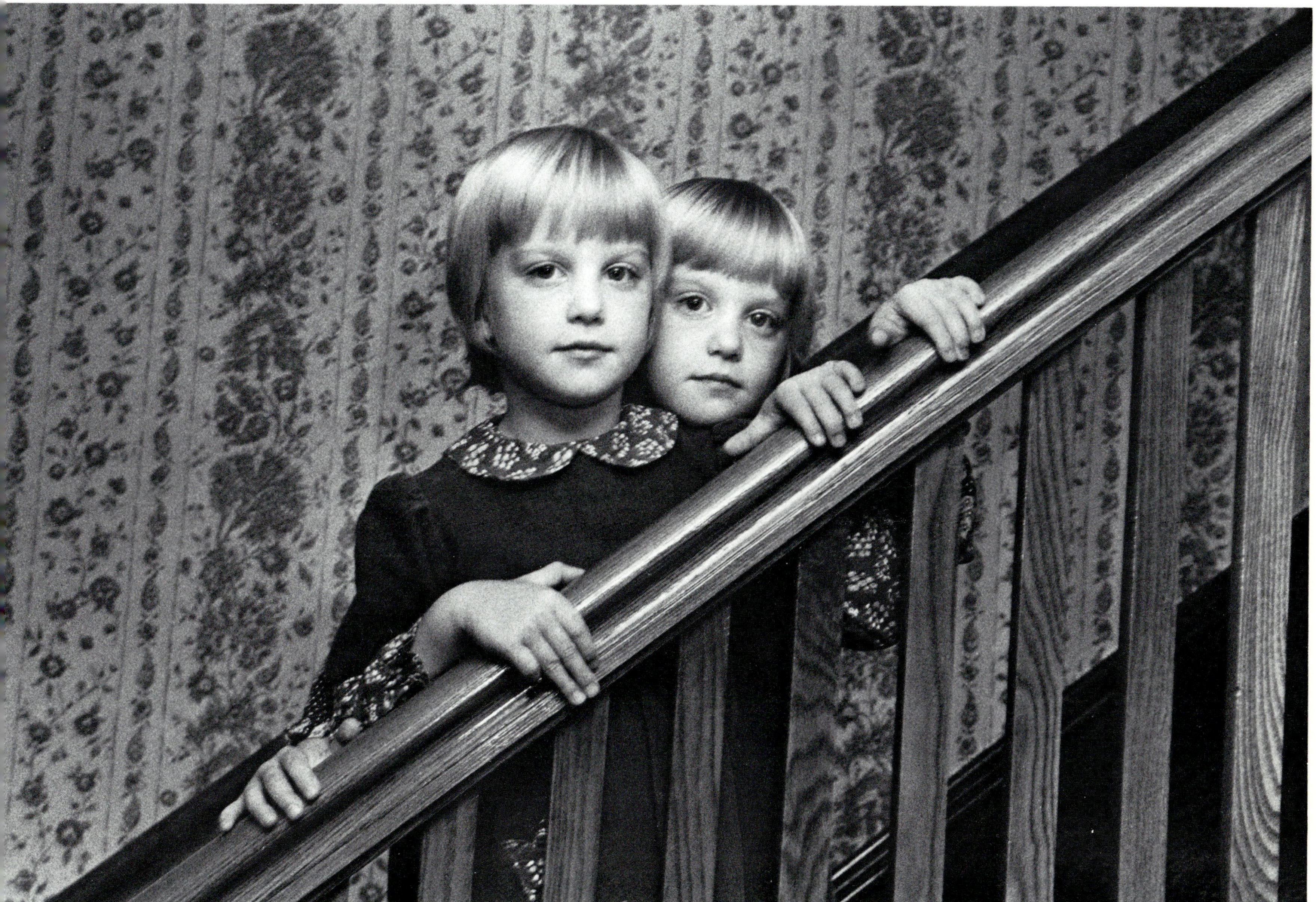

Nine-year-old Puerto Rican Albino Twins, Brooklyn, New York
 "It's not twins that are strange but, rather, it's the way people react to twins that is strange."

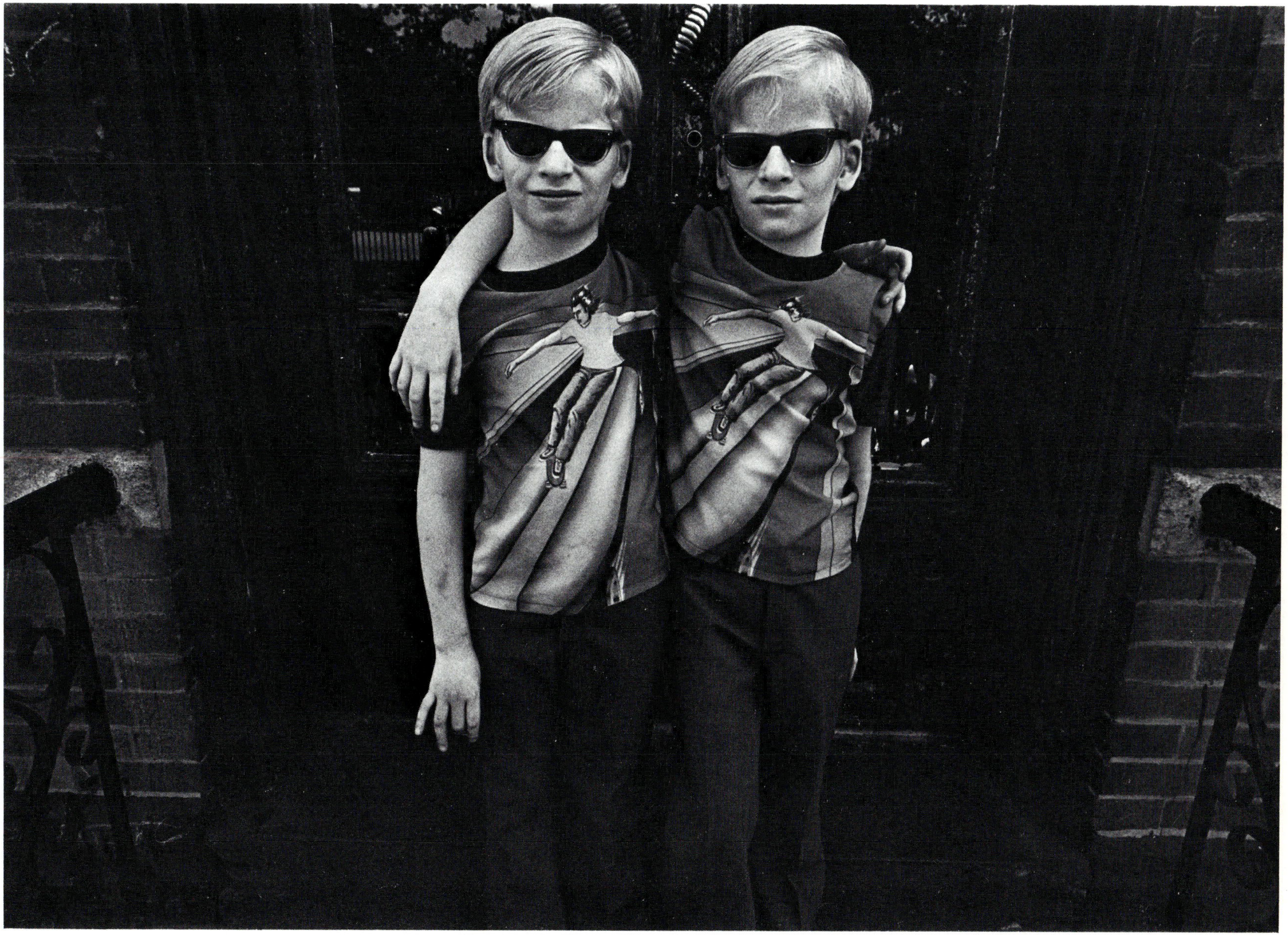

"If we did something wrong and Mother wanted to punish us, she'd scold and hit us both without ever trying to find out which one was to blame."

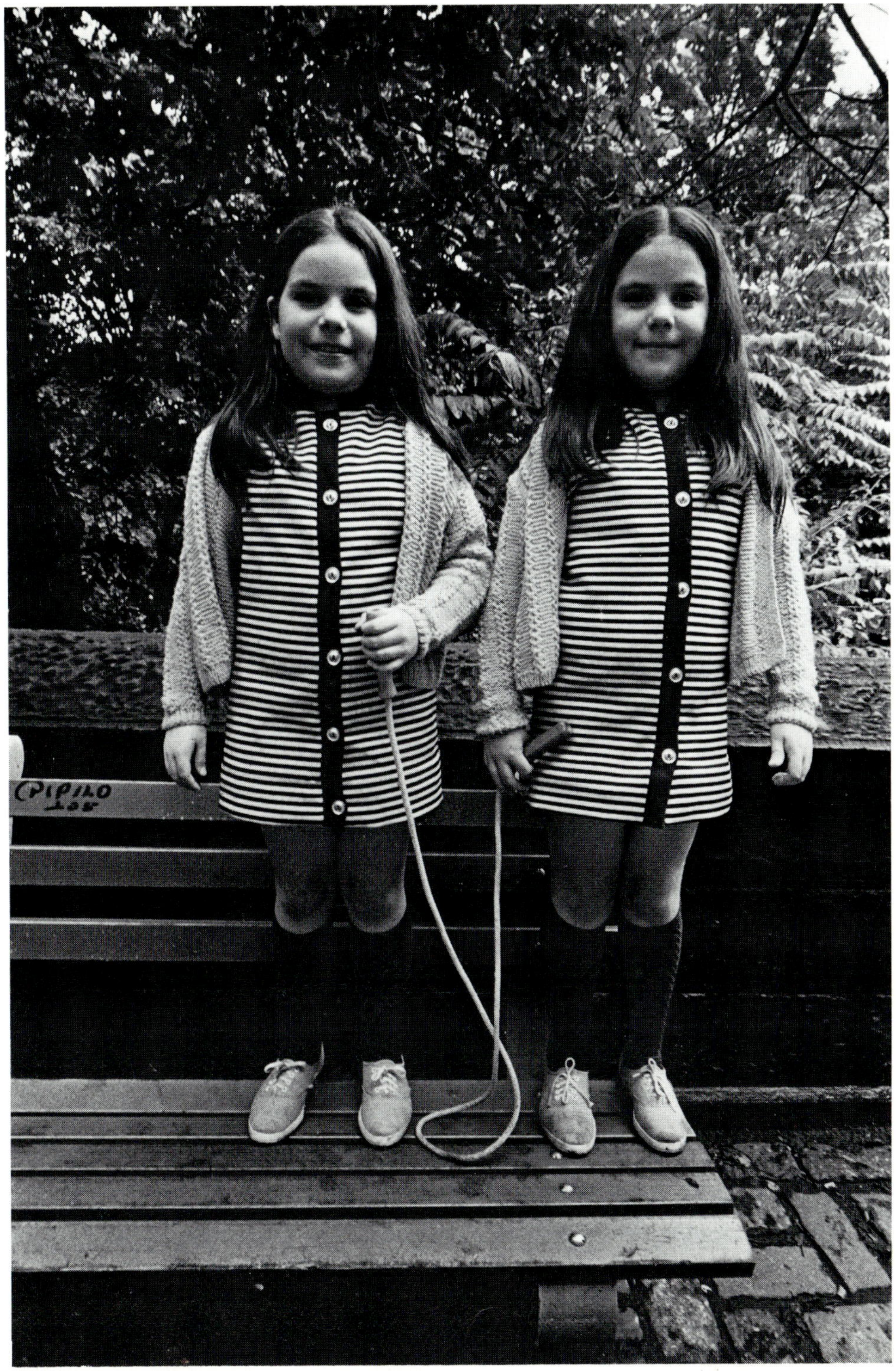

Mother of Twins:

"Sometimes I can't tell my twin boys apart. This hurts me. A name comes off my tongue so fast. They correct me but I can hear the hurt in their voices. This is especially true if they are telling me something important. Their father never attempts to call them by their first name—he just calls them the twinners."

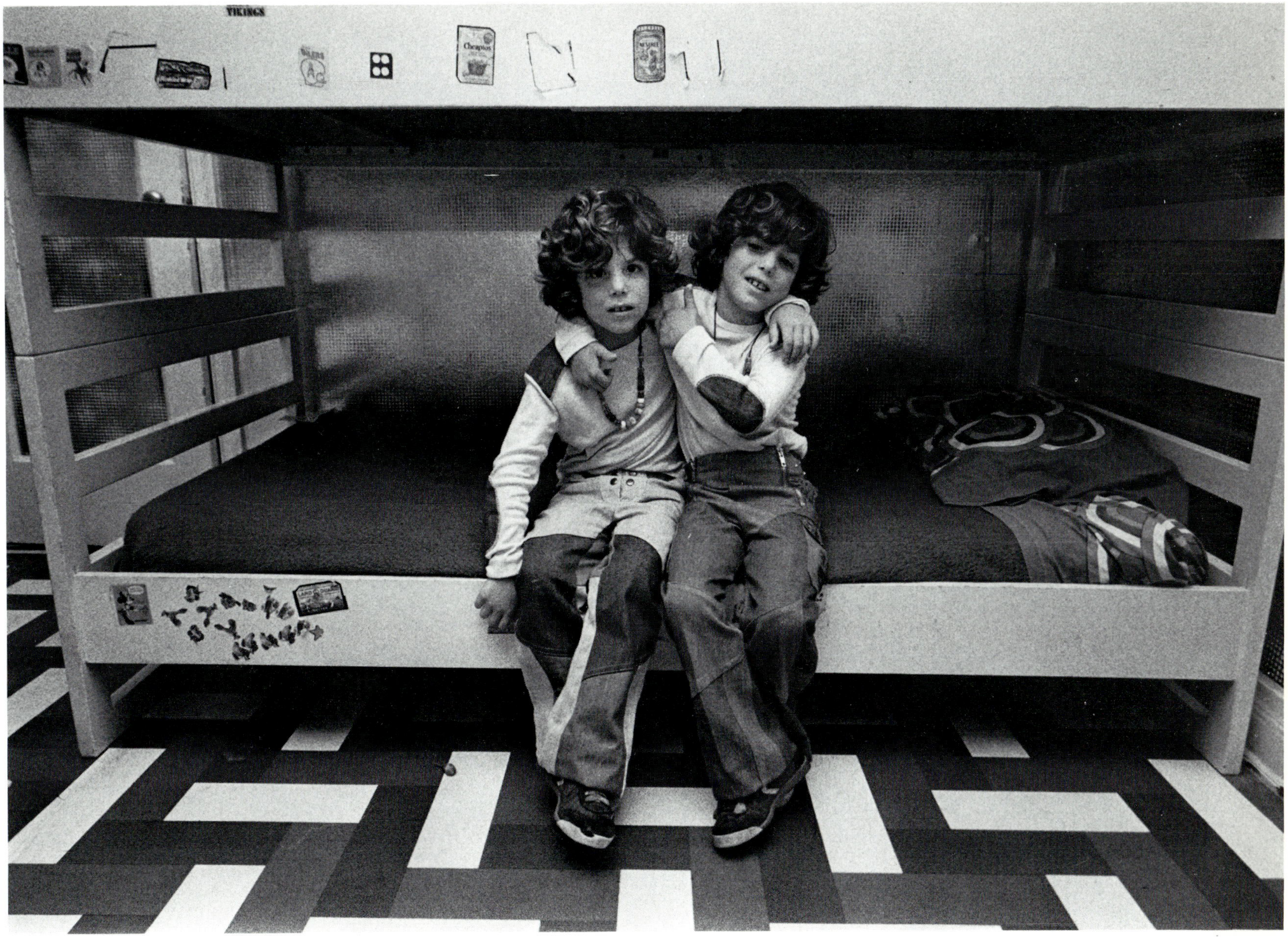

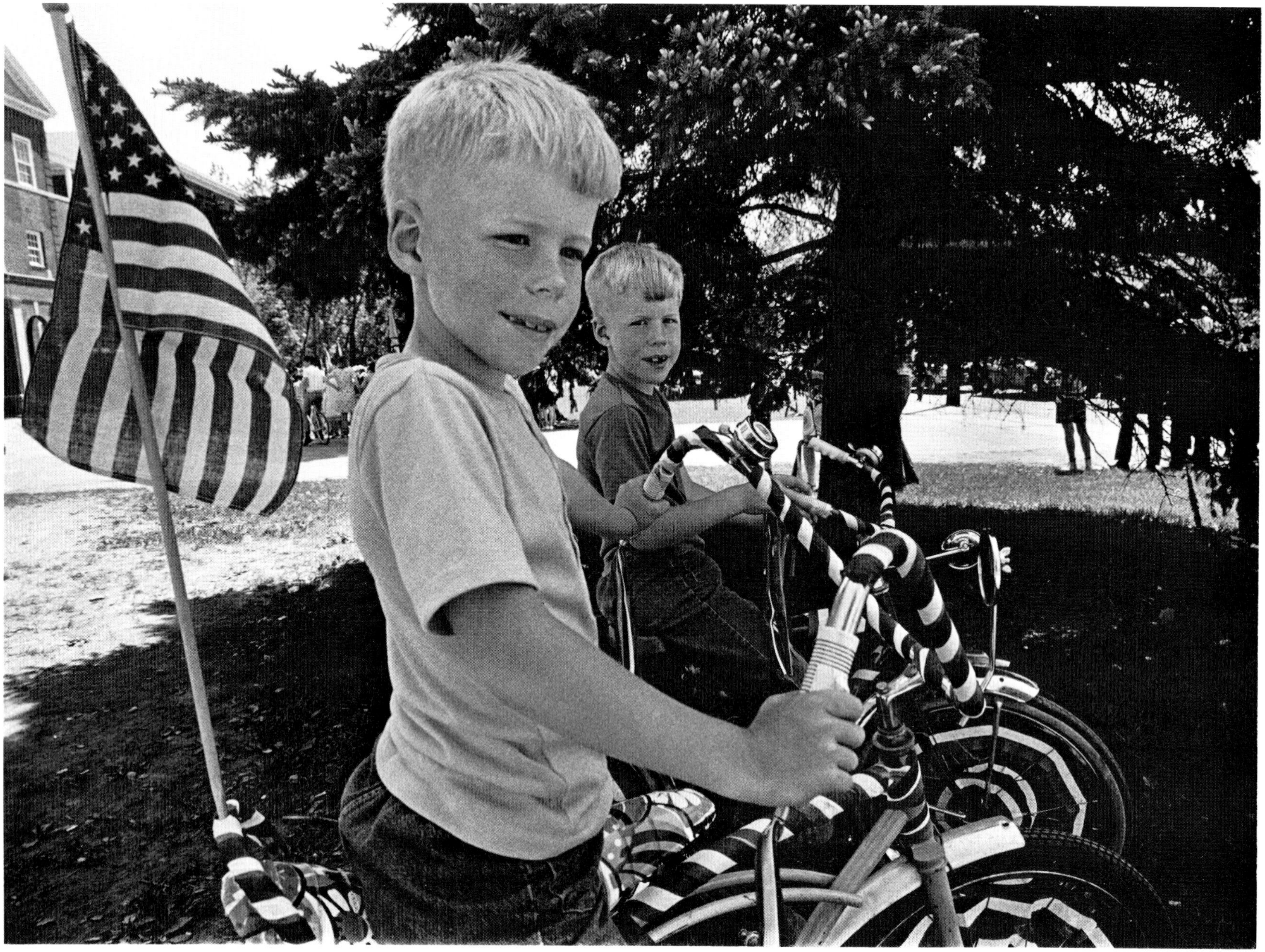

"When our parents had guests, we were usually brought out, put under a floor lamp and scrutinized. They studied our hand lines, picked us up to see who weighed more, and tried to tell us apart. It was like a game; we didn't mind at all."

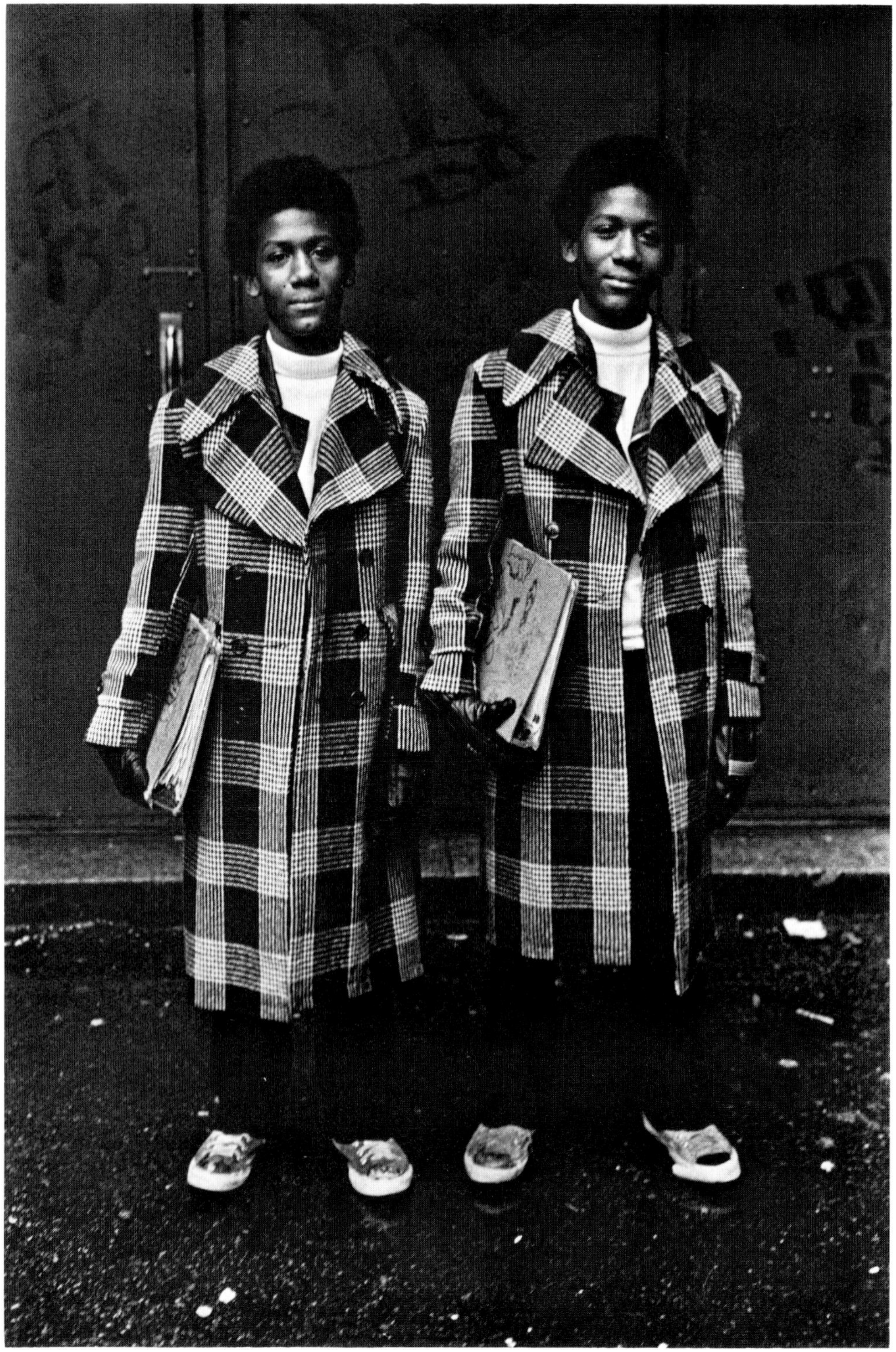

MOTHER OF TWINS:

"My boys used to love being twins and being dressed alike. But one day they came home from school, threw their books across the floor, and said they'd never dress alike again. Their classmates taunted them for being the Bobbsey Twins. One thing that will split a set of twins up faster than anything else is when their classmates start calling them freaks."

"Our brother, who is four years older than we are, claims that when we were born, he lost his identity and status. He was devastated by our birth. He is always known as the twins' brother and everybody forgets his name."

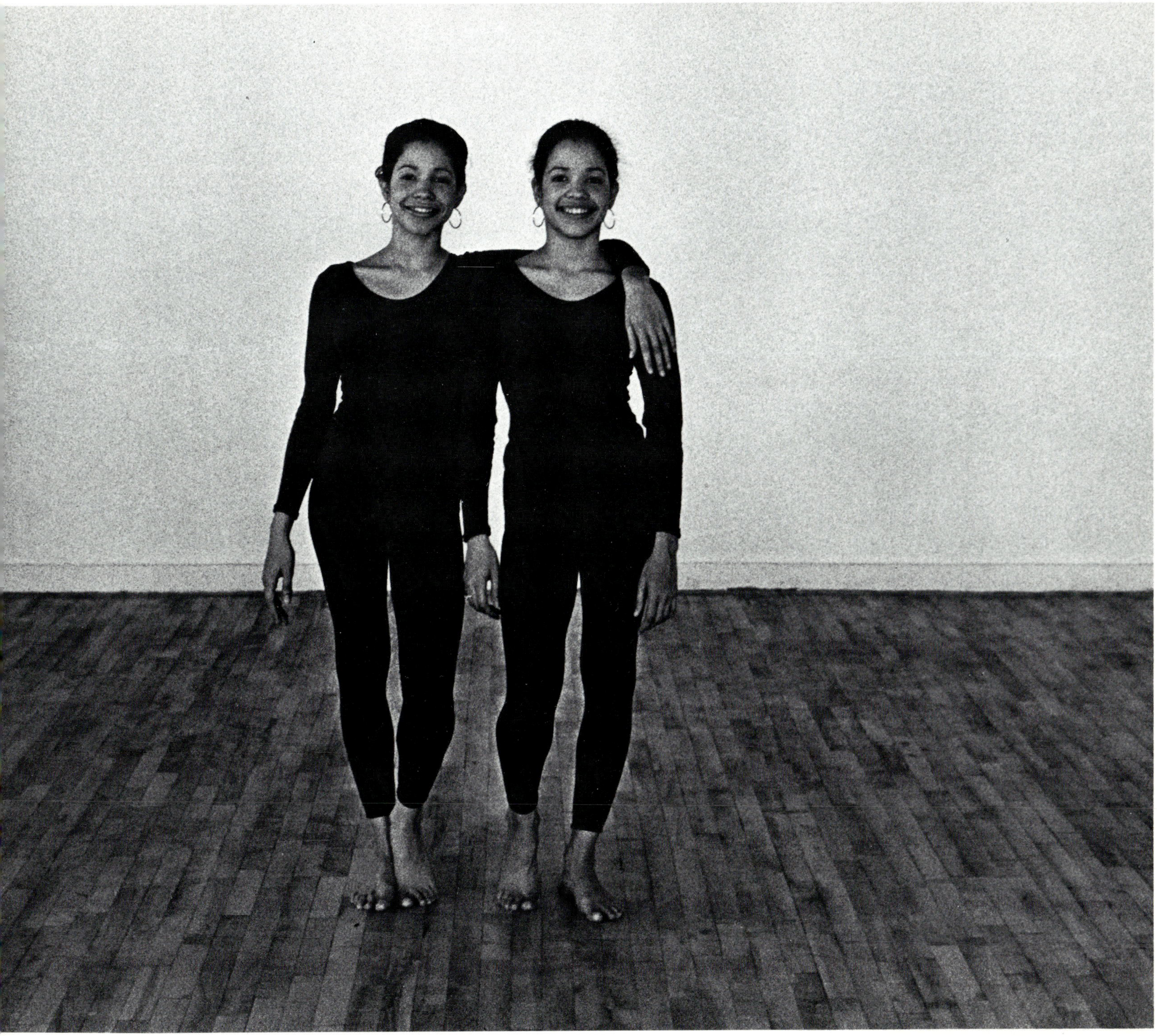

"Anything I can do my twin can do as well. No better and no worse."

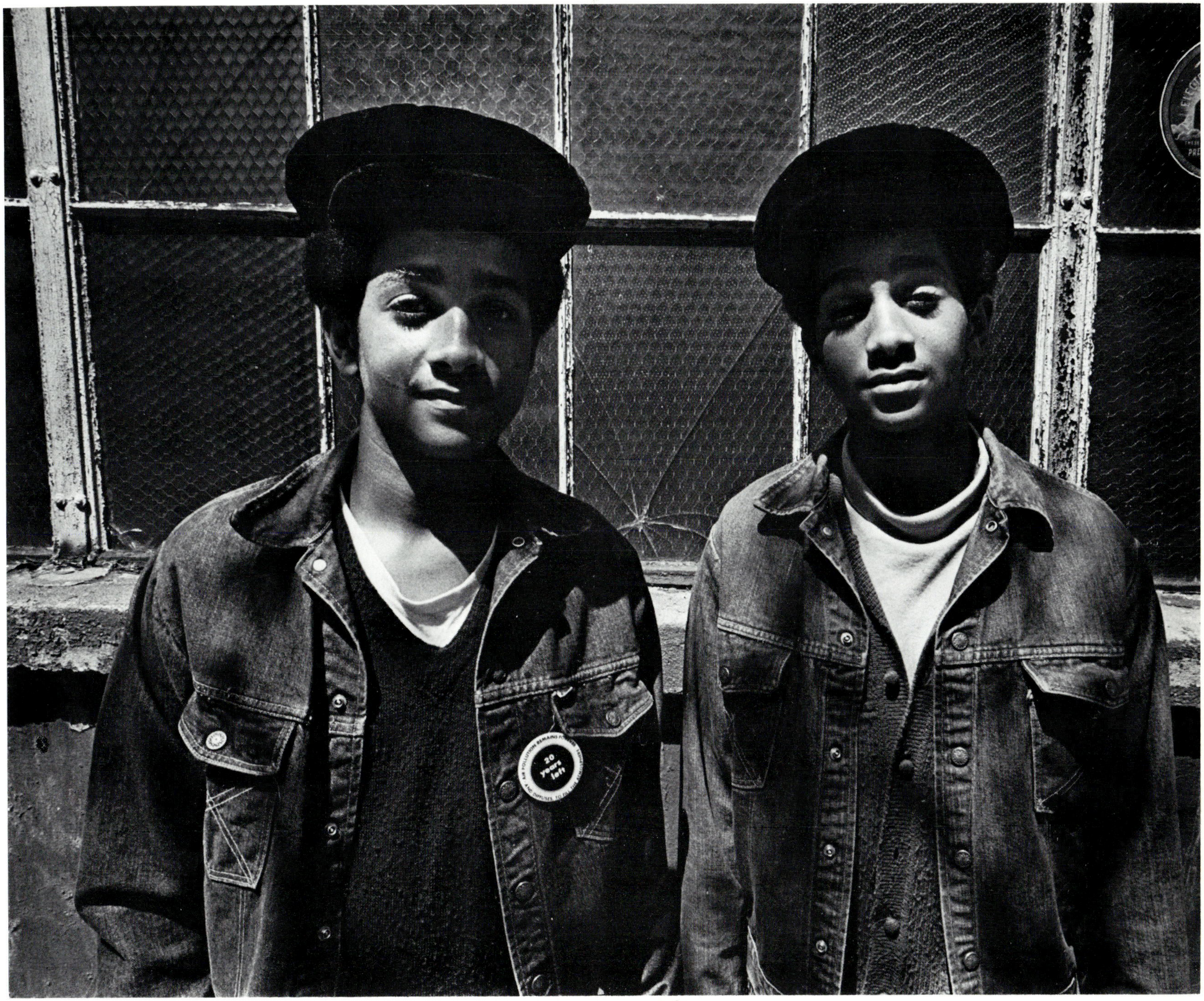
20
years
left

"I used to wake up in the morning and see my twin in her bed and think, 'How do I know I am me?'"

"If someone calls out my twin's name, I naturally answer."

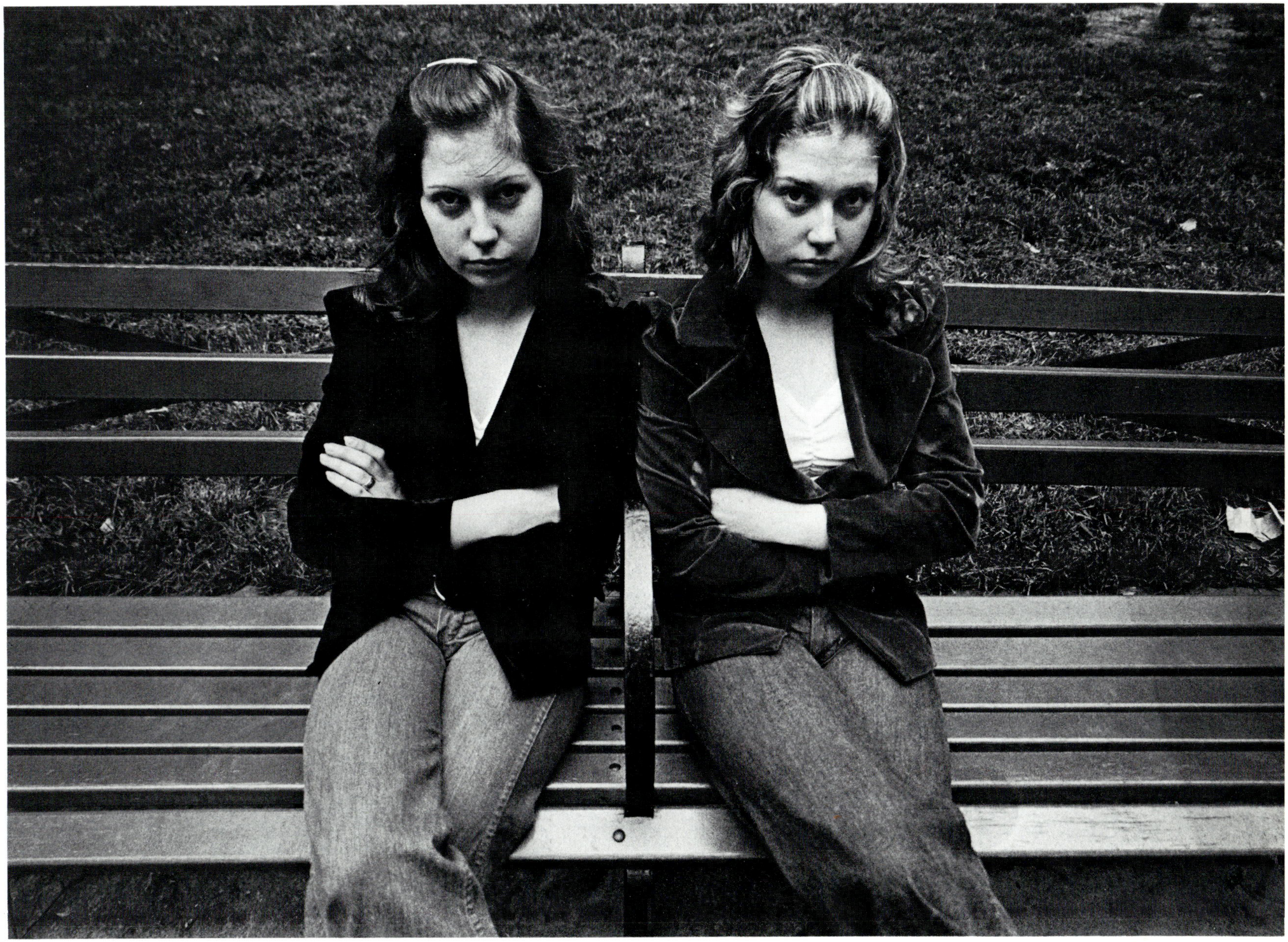

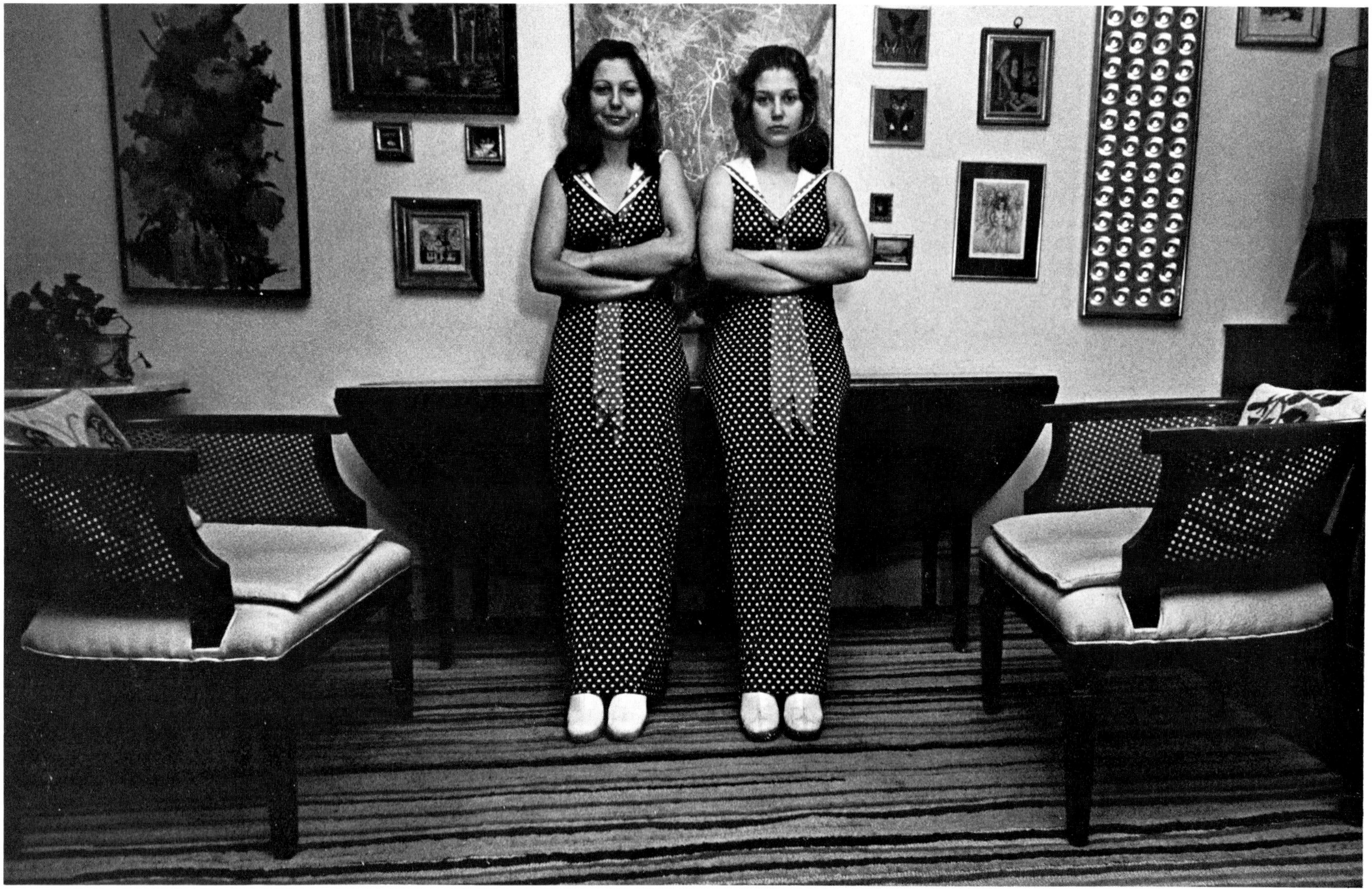

"My sister fell down a flight of stairs in high school and injured her appendix. When they came to tell me this in class, they found me on the floor in pain. When the doctors took her into surgery, I could tell the exact moment when they started cutting and when they sewed her up. I was in the waiting room with Mother. She said, 'Well, the operation should be over by now,' and I said, 'No, Mother, the doctor just started.' And, indeed, the doctor later verified to us that the operation had been delayed."

Kem:

"We couldn't switch dummies. I can't make Rufus's personality come out like Kern can. When I get my dummy out and look at his face, it just comes to life and I'm not even aware that I am the one doing it."

Kern:

"Each dummy has its own unique personality, with a face that kind of matches that personality. Rufus is the down-home, country type. He appears dumb but isn't. He's insulting but likes girls. Randy is shy, smart, and inward. If we had twin dummies, they wouldn't have very different personalities and the audience would probably think they are the same. In a sense, not having twin dummies is a way of protecting a part of ourselves, part of what I feel is uniquely me as compared to what it is that joins us together as twins."

Kem:

"A psychiatrist came up to us after seeing our act and said that we were bringing out a part of ourselves through the dummies that we couldn't bring out by ourselves. He felt that the dummies matched us and that their personalities were repressed parts of us. We've come to see the truth in what he said."

(*left*) Kern with "Rufus";   (*right*) Kem with "Randy"

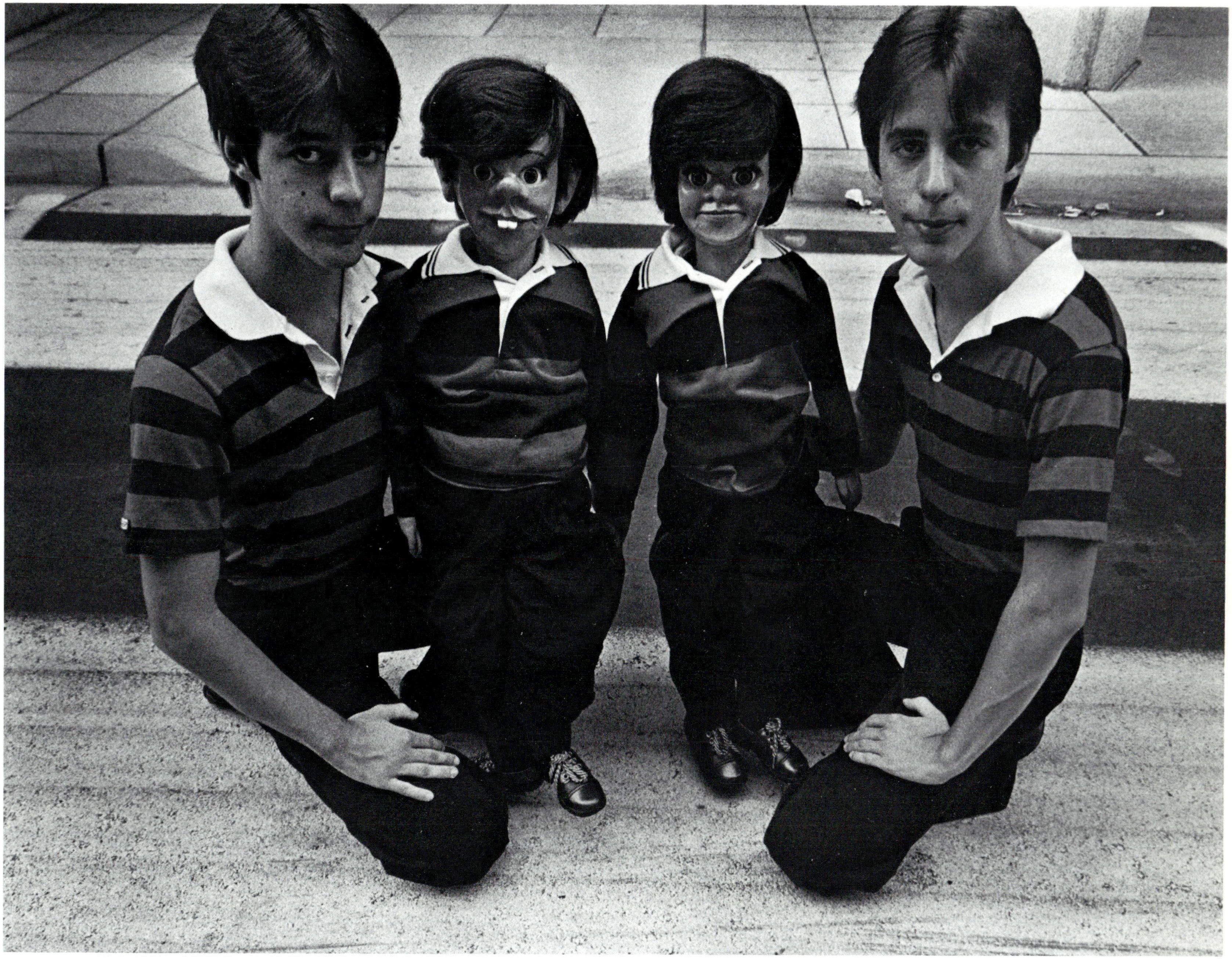

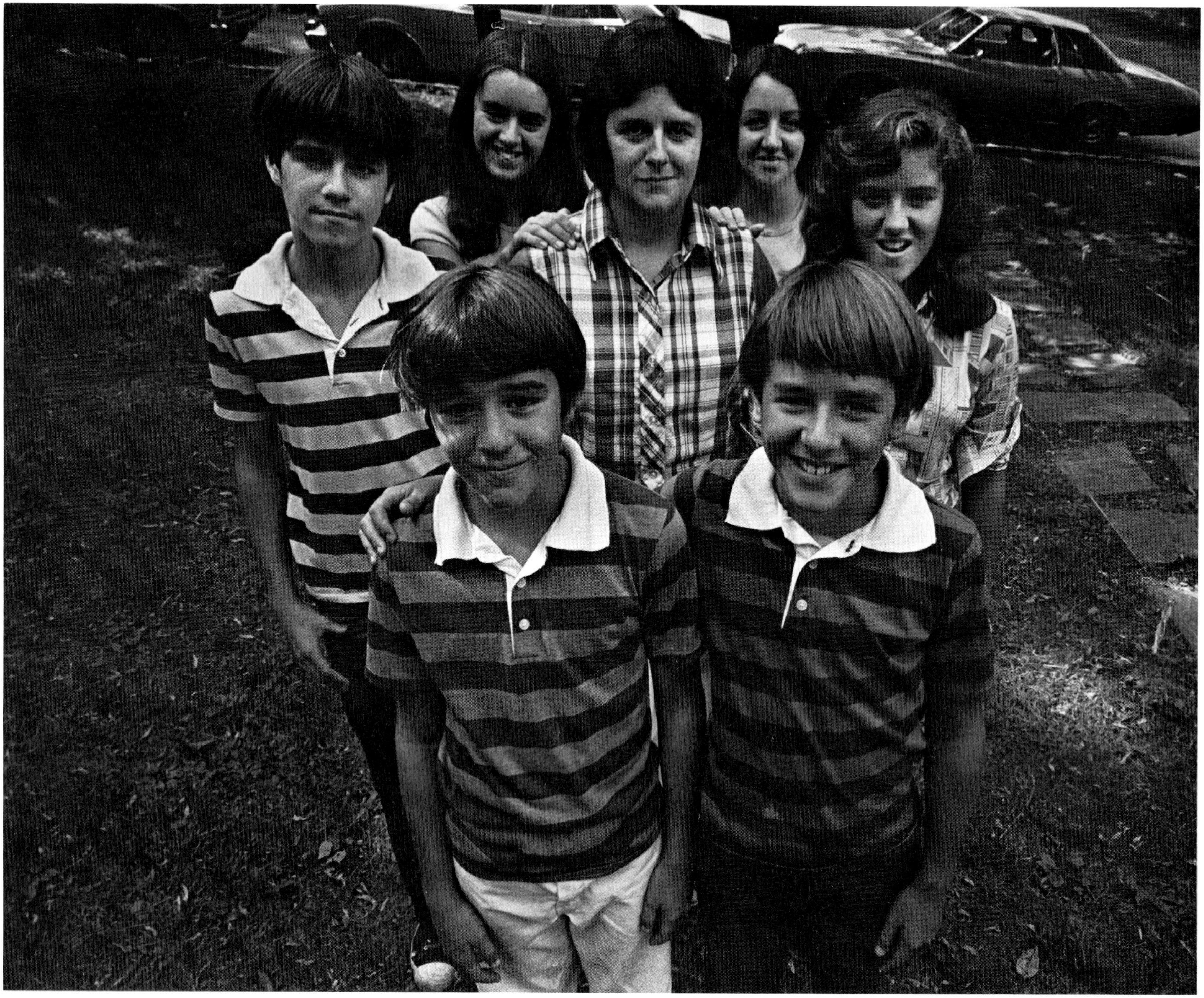

Mother of Three Sets of Twins:

"I was thrilled to have the first set of twins. I thought it was special; not everyone could have twins. Then I had two miscarriages that were twins. After the first miscarriage, we began to wonder. My husband asked the doctor whether I could ever have a single birth and he said I could only have multiple births. An insurance executive told us he computed the odds of having three sets of twins as one in five million births.

"I felt that same specialness at the birth of the second and third set of twins. By the third set, we hoped it would be twin boys so we'd have three boys and three girls. By that time, it would have been very *odd* if I had given birth to a single child.

"We didn't make a conscious effort to stop having children once the third set of twins were born. Even though we knew we'd have at least twins. Whatever came, came."

Oldest Set of Twins:

"We don't think of ourselves or our brothers and sisters as twins. It's just that there are two of each."

Mother:

"I know they are twins medically and physically but I don't pair them off. It's just six individual, healthy kids. This is the way I wanted them to be. I didn't want them singled out as twins. Everyone always looks at twins and makes them feel strange and I'm sure they do the same with my children. But I want to keep that to a minimum.

"We were told that it was not too good to dress them alike or encourage them to be too dependent on each other. Our doctor told us that we'd have trouble with the twin girls if we kept them in the same school. And sure enough, one of them started to act strangely; she began to have nightmares and it turned out that this was because she didn't have as many friends as her twin sister."

"My twin has been my brother and friend when we were infants, growing up, and now. Whereas other friends come and go, I know he will be my friend forever and that's very nice."

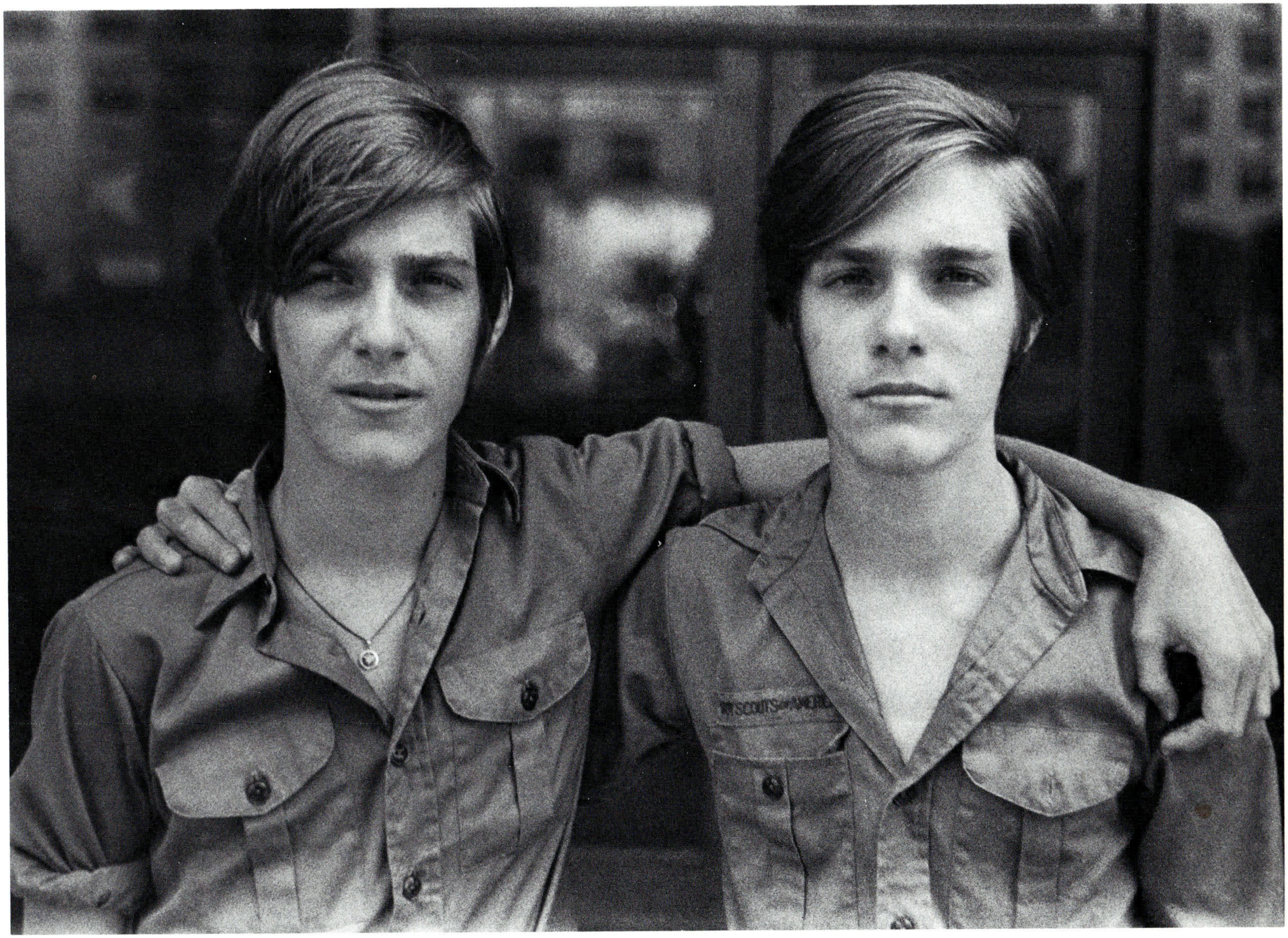

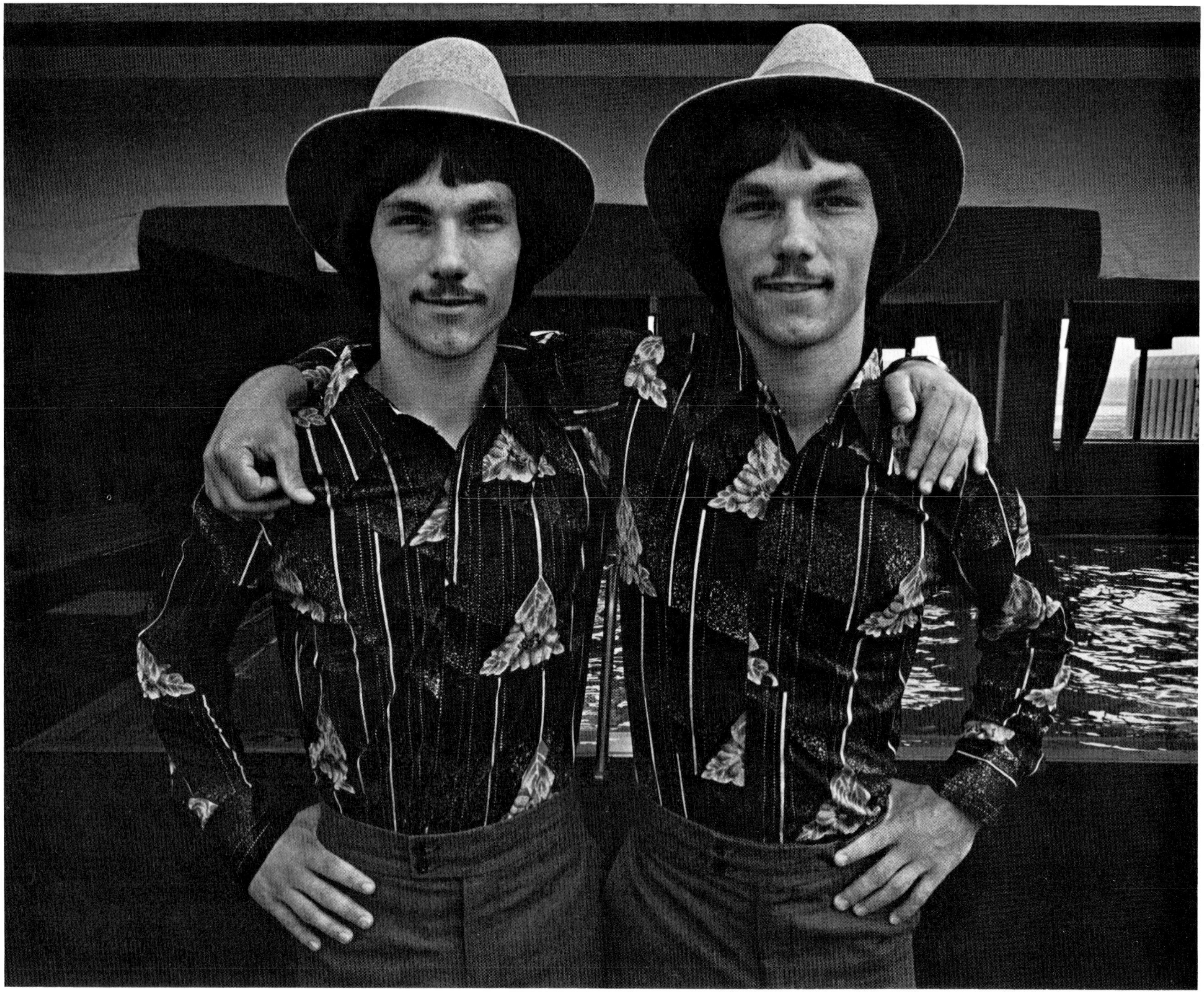

"We were always lumped together and treated as just another object by our mother. She would introduce us to her friends by saying, 'This is my son.'"

A Non-Twin:
"I'm glad I'm not a twin because I want to be unique. I'd rather stand alone than share my accomplishments, achievements, and even my failures. I don't want to be compared to anyone. I want to be recognized for me. I think I would feel misunderstood if I were a twin; I'd feel that people would be into my physical appearance and not really *me*."

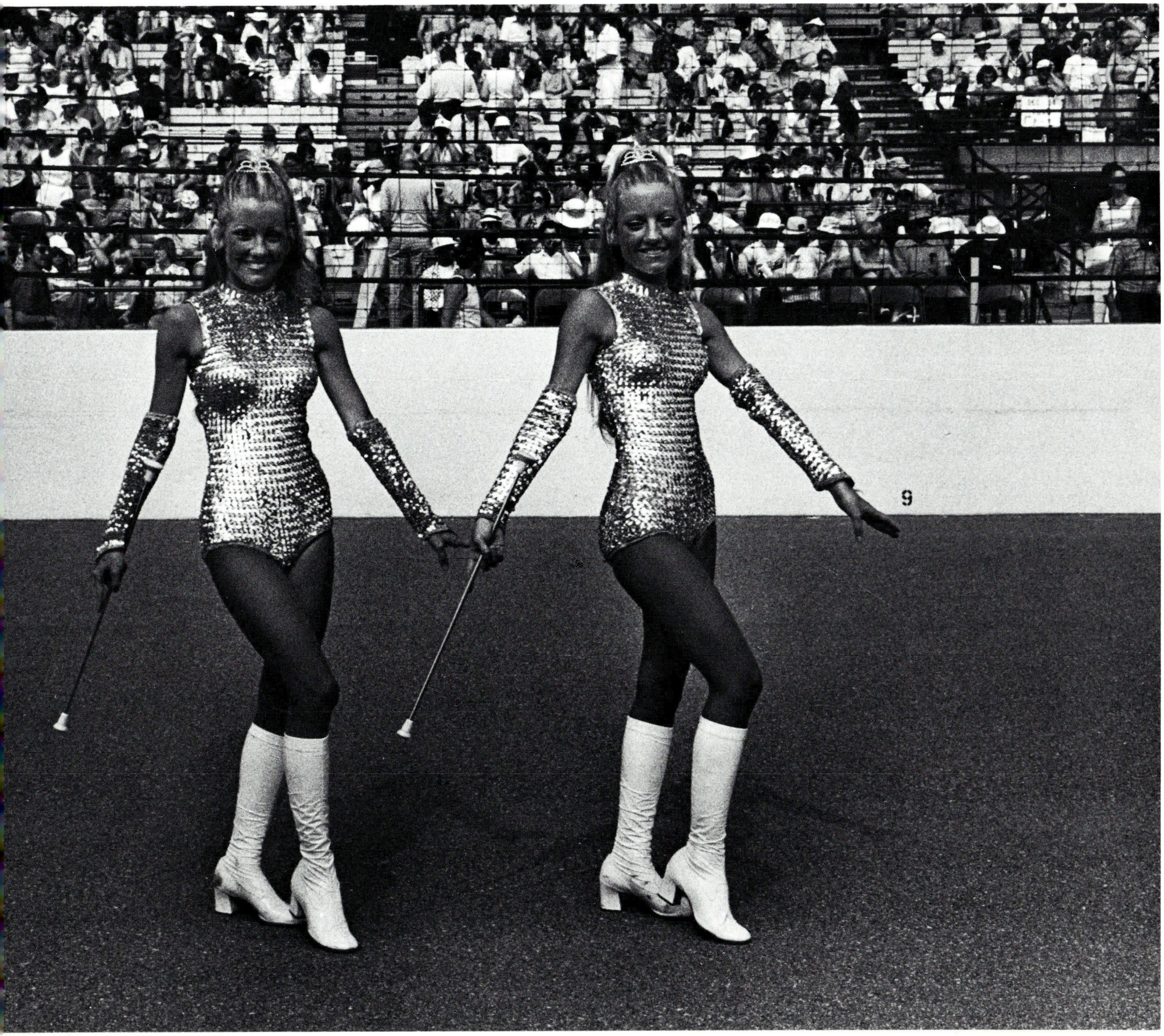
9

A Local News Dispatch in a New England Newspaper:

"Academic honors were issued in duplicate for Peter and Paul ———. Both were elected to Phi Beta Kappa at the University of Vermont. Both received bachelor of arts degrees with honors in English, their major field. Both were named the outstanding senior English major. Both won a fellowship for graduate study, which both intend to use at the same graduate school, where both will continue in English. Perhaps to break the monotony, Paul graduated *summa cum laude* and Peter, *magna cum laude*."

Peter and Paul are constantly harassed because of their names. They are called Pete and Repete; St. Peter and St. Paul; Peter Paul Almond; Peter, Paul and Mary. "We each like our names individually, but, as a pair, the names are painful. We wish our parents had named us David and George or something very dissimilar." Peter says, "I treasure my middle initial because it is different than Paul's."

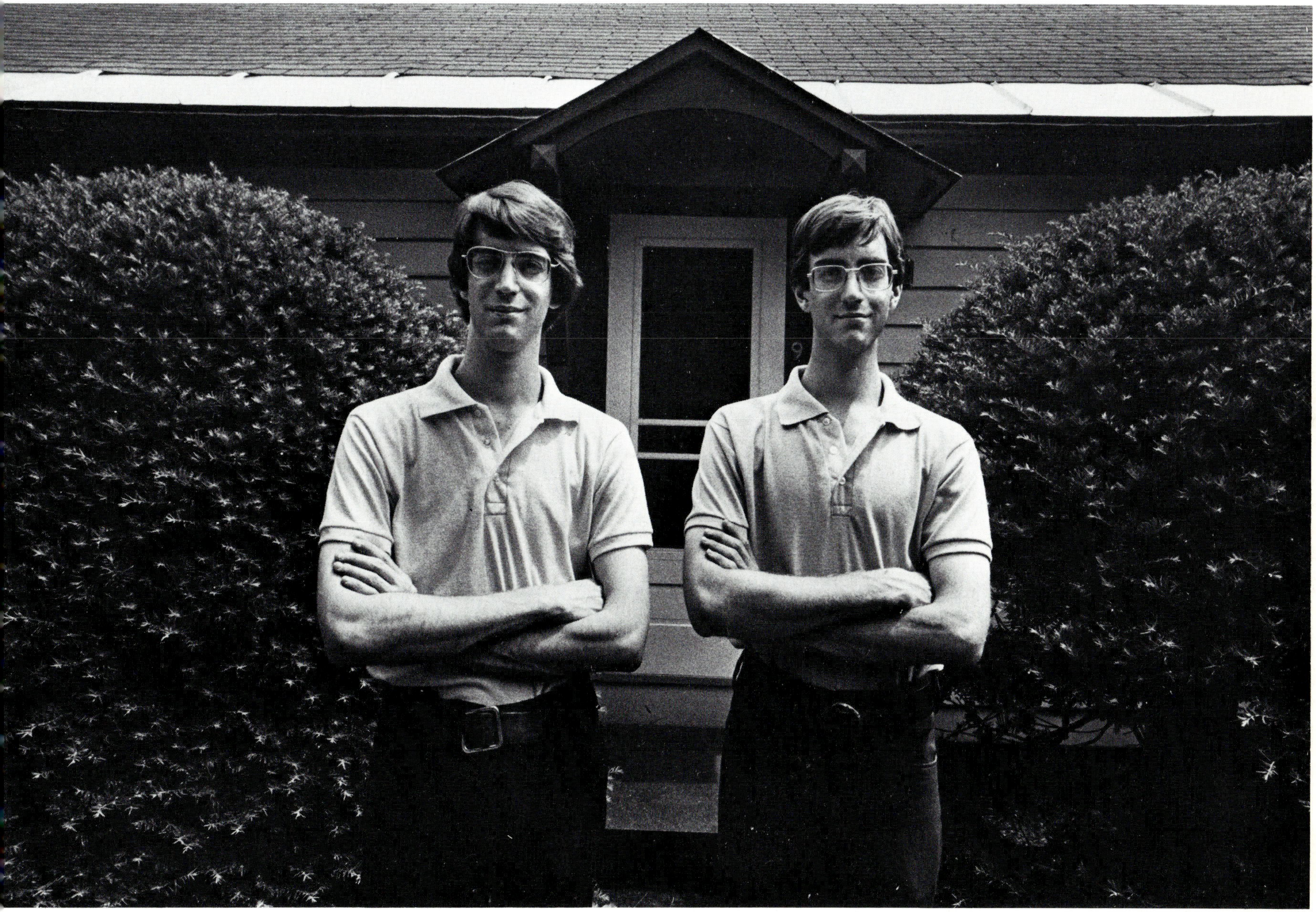

"To this day, our father calls us 'Sis.' He's never called us by our real names. It makes me believe that he has never known who we really are."

"Somewhere as a child I heard a tale that one of a pair of twins could not have children. I was always afraid it would be me."

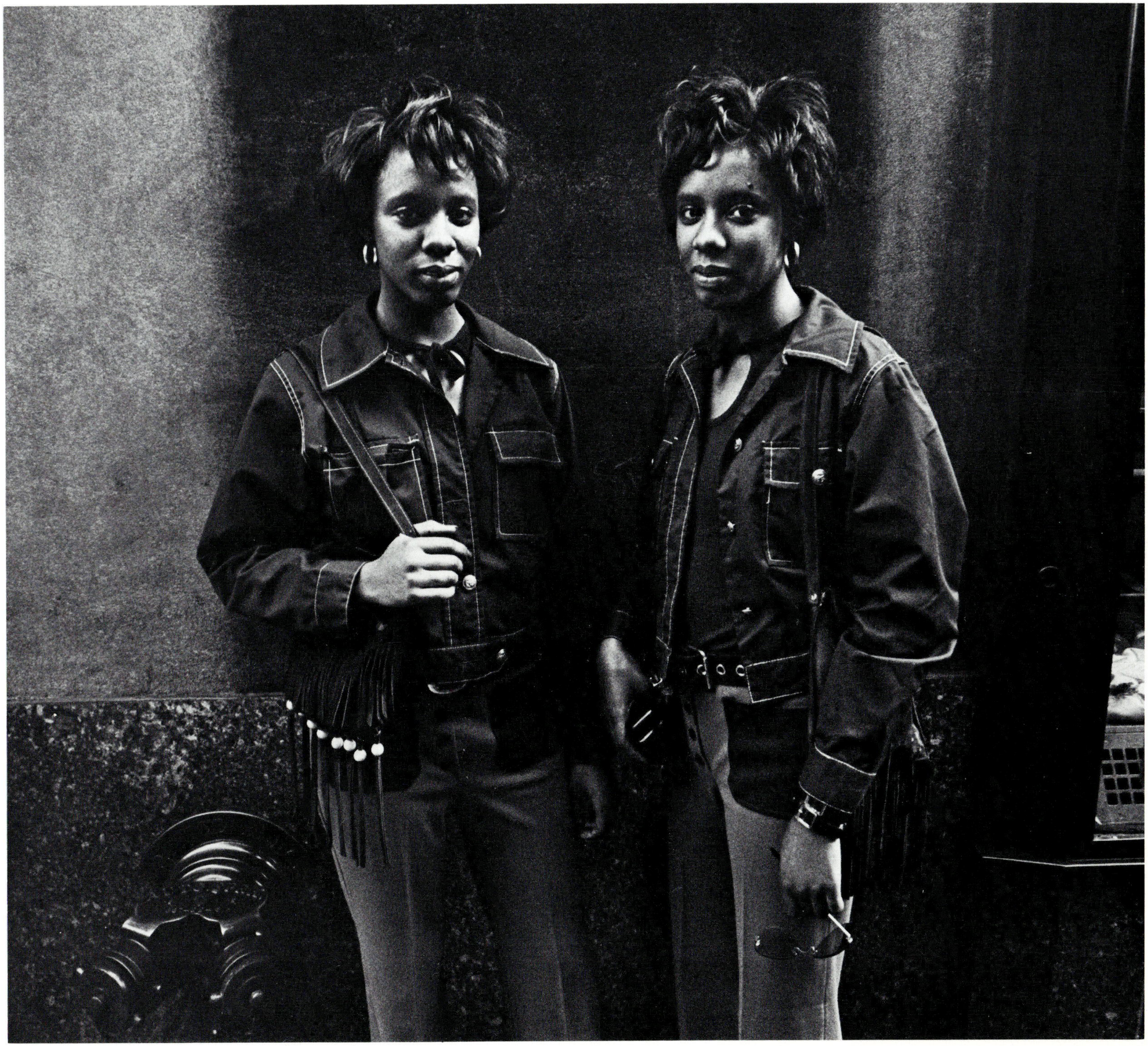

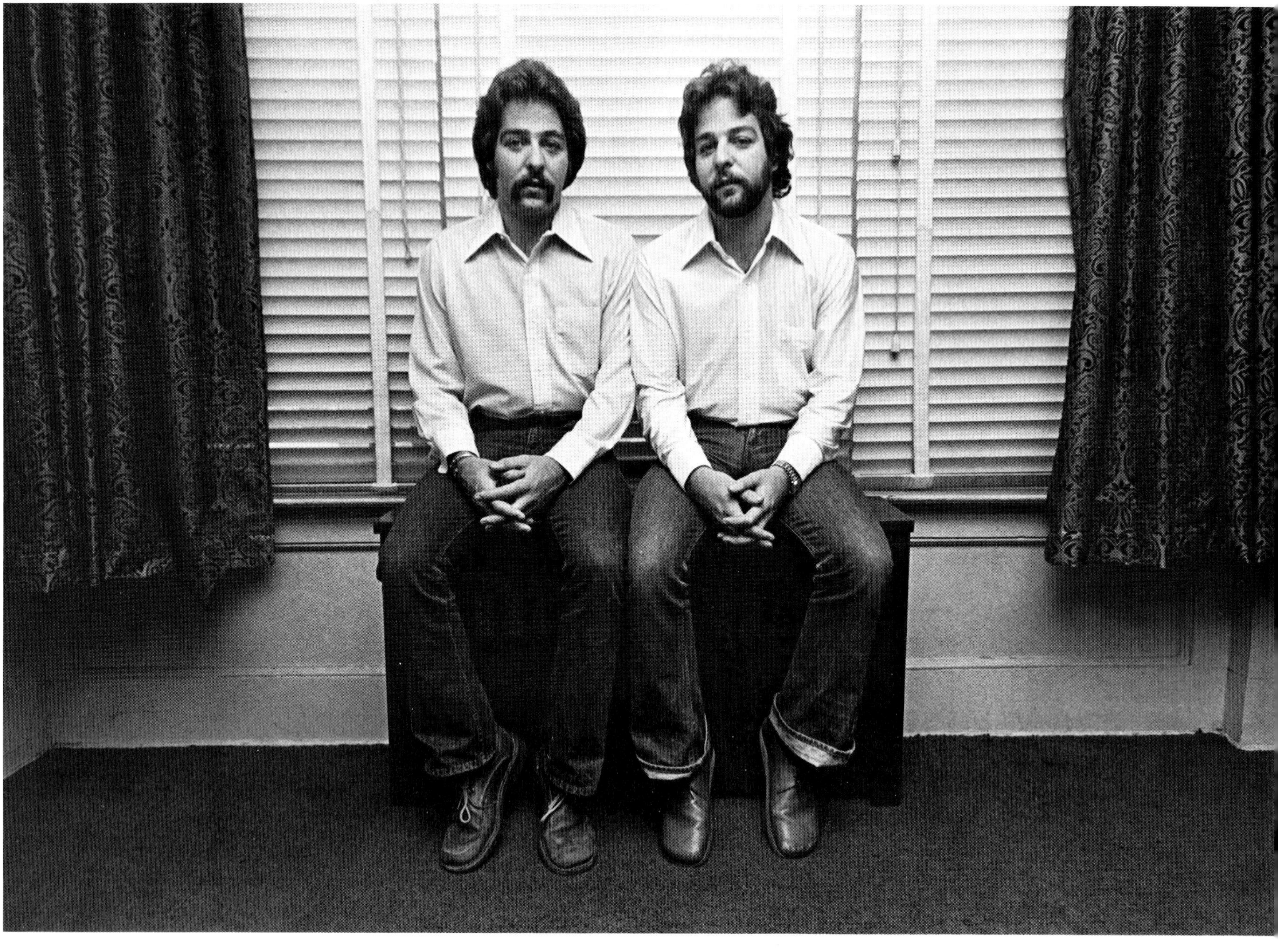

"My twin is my confidant. There isn't anything that I'm involved in that he isn't also involved in or doesn't know about."

"As a teenager, I became aware that my family, friends, and peers viewed me very much as they did my twin. I never stopped and thought at any one point, 'Hey, I'm a twin but I should still be an individual.' It came to me gradually. But when I fully realized it, I was worried and even horrified. From then on, I never dressed like her. In fact, I made a strong effort to be as different from her as possible."

"Being a twin is like having a walking mirror."

"We complement and expand each other beyond what we could accomplish alone."

"If I were not a twin, I'd probably be married with children now."

"We have exactly the same characteristics as one, because we are one."

"I can emulate my twin because I respect and see good in him."

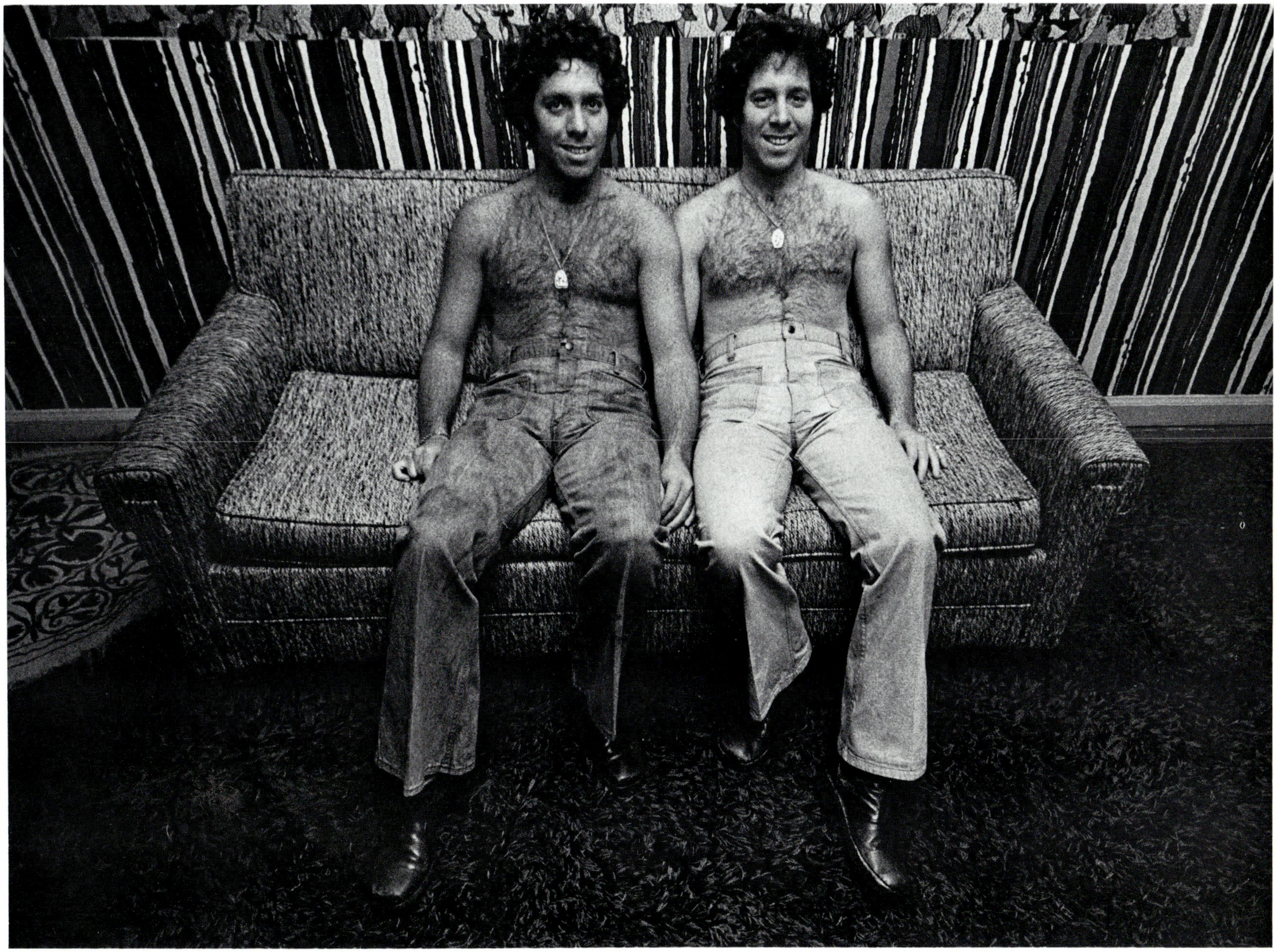

Twin Stewardesses Who Always Fly Together:
"We hate to fly in 727s. There isn't enough room in them and the work load is usually very hectic. The only good thing about the plane is that it has double jump seats so we can sit together when we take off and land. This way, we'll be together if we crash and probably both survive or perish together. We think about this often."

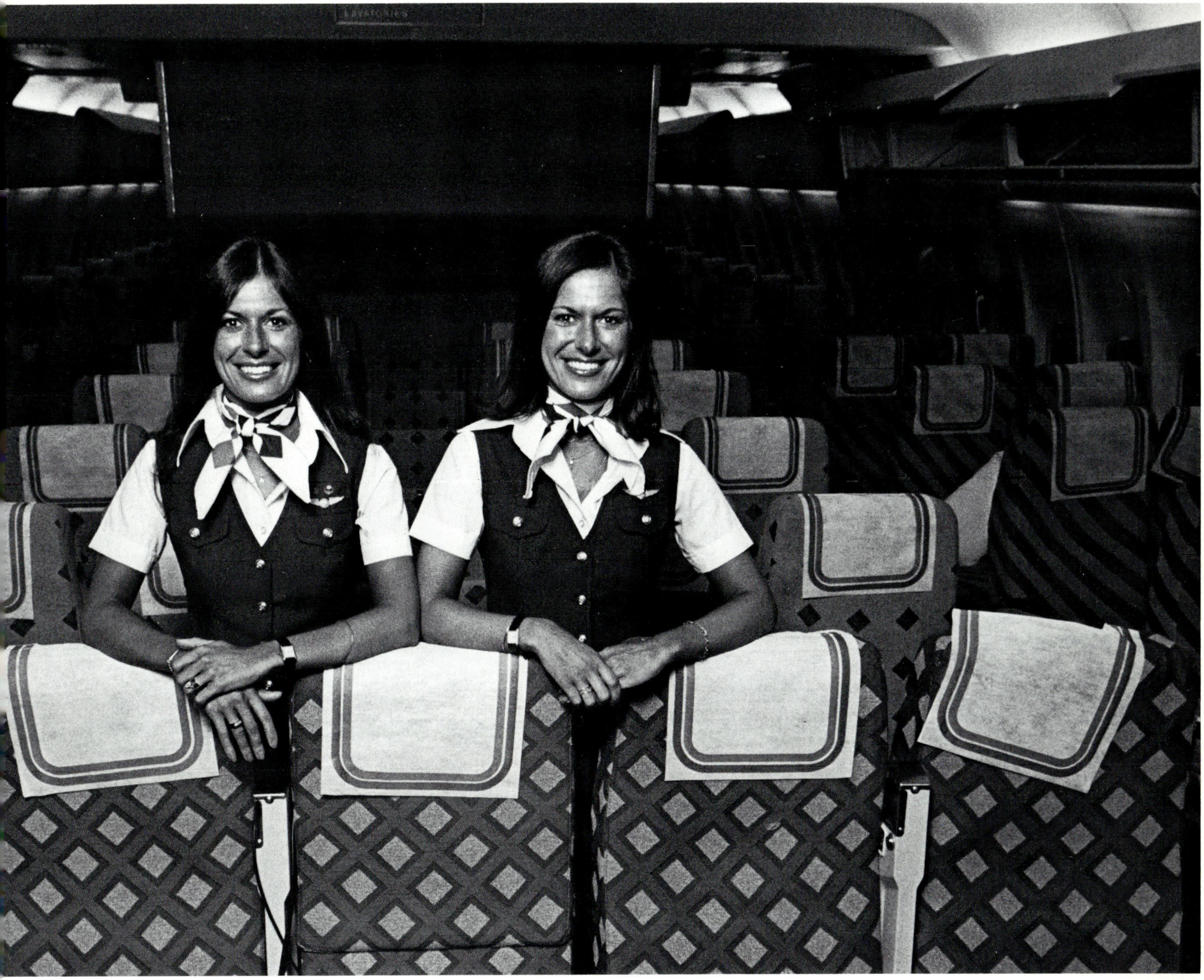

A WHEY WITH CURDS
FROZEN FANTASIES
SOFT FLUFFY YOGURT SERVED WITH NATURAL DELIGHTS !
TOPLESS
LARGE
REGULAR
TOPPED
LARGE
REGULAR
TOPPINGS: FRESH FRUIT
GARNISHES
LIME
CHOCOLATE
ALL SHOOK UP!
ATURAL FROZEN YOGURT MILK SHAKES !
MOCHA-YOGA
THE YO GOAT FLOAT
SPECIAL TREATS: TAKE-HOME PACKAGES · PARFAITS
PARTY CAKES · YOGURT WHEYFERS
CURDS 'N'
CURDS 'N'

"I've been told all my life that I have to be different from my brother. But how can I change something that is always there—something I was born with? I have a closeness and a feeling and a bond that individuals do not have. I may try to look different and try to learn different things, but that bond is still there drawing us together. What can I do about it? I can't break it unless I slice the other half off, and I can't do that."

"We were together at birth. What could be a closer bond? We must have taught each other how to talk; even now we have our own special vocabulary and personal culture. And we feel together even when separated."

"The biggest change in our lives occurred when we went away to different colleges. We were aware of our strong dependency on each other and made a conscious effort to break the ties; it was an inevitability that we knew had to come and college seemed a good point to initiate the separation. It was a very difficult time. When I saw my twin for the first time since going away, I cried. The hardest time was on our birthday—it was very strange and sad celebrating a birthday without the person who shared my birth. It was just not the same."

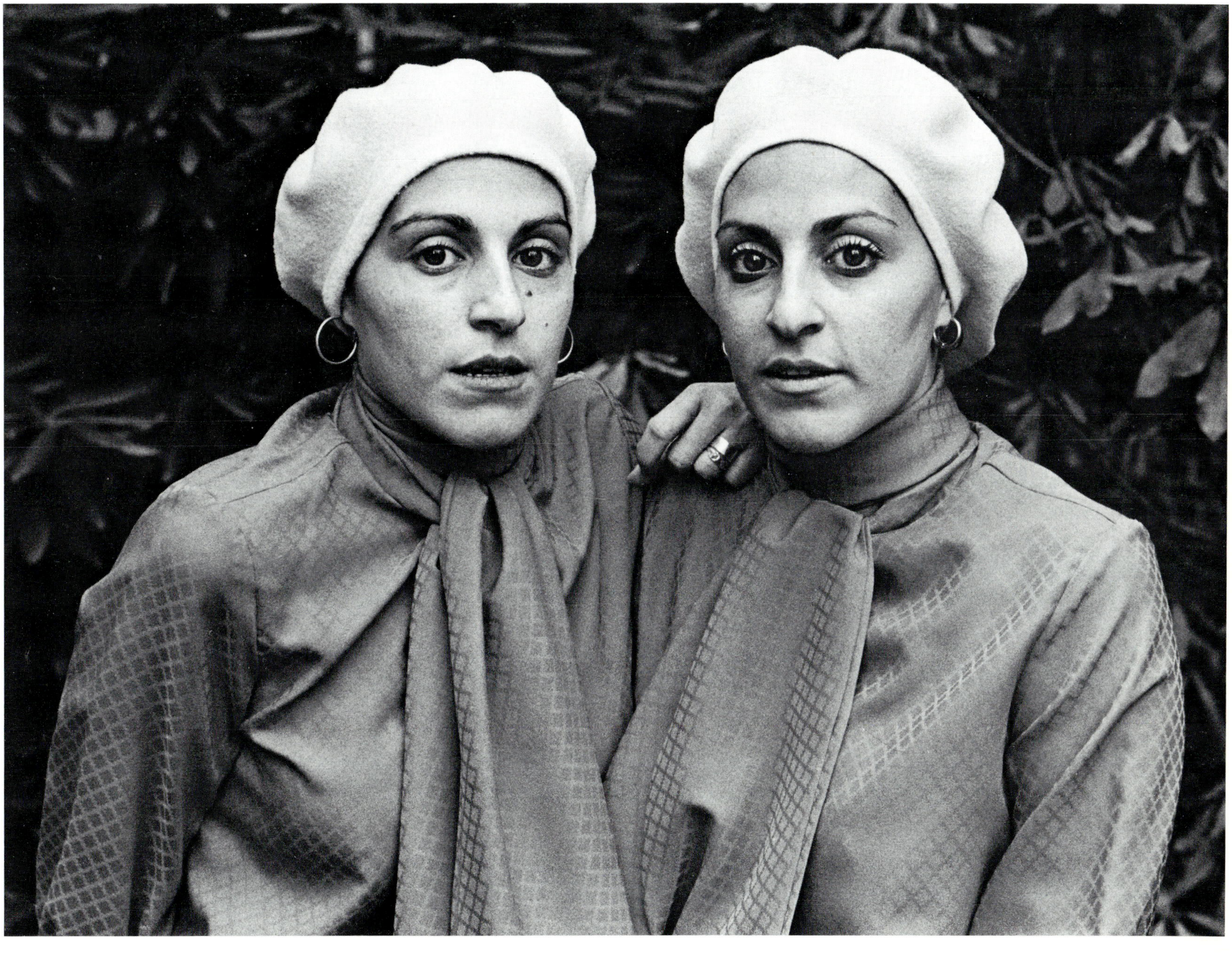

"We won a three-legged race when we were fourteen years old. That really sealed our partnership—we realized that we were better as a pair than as individuals."

"My twin and I never had a strong sense of personal property. Even now we keep our clothes in a 'collective' closet. We don't individually own clothes; they are all shared and worn by me and my twin—the same pants, shirts, even underwear and shoes."

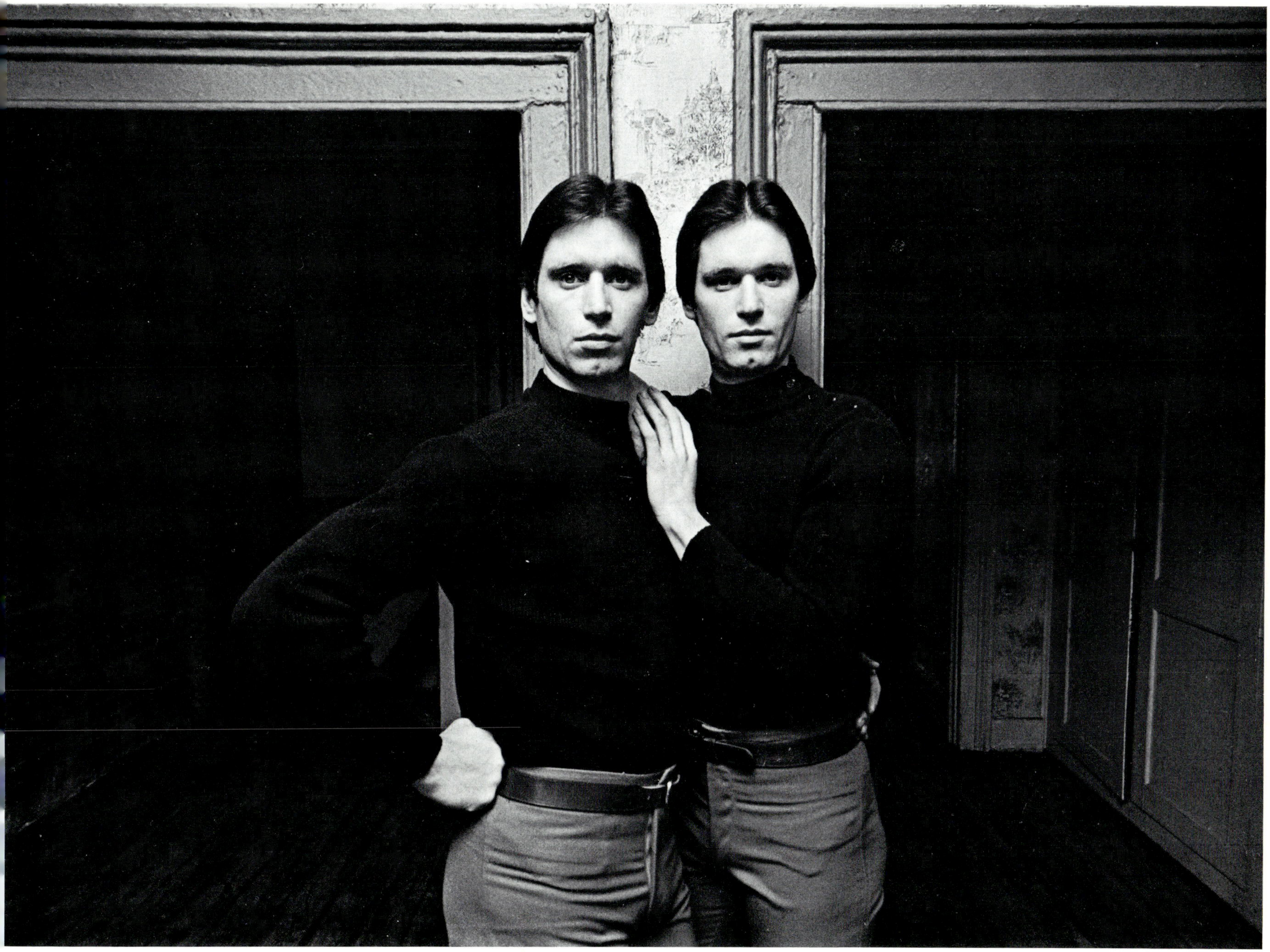

"I can't think of myself as me. I'm always comparing myself to my twin."

"I have always thought that my twin is more interesting than I am."

"My twin is more my competition than my friend."

"As a nine-year-old, being a twin meant I was never lonely. As a thirty-year-old, it means that I am never left alone."

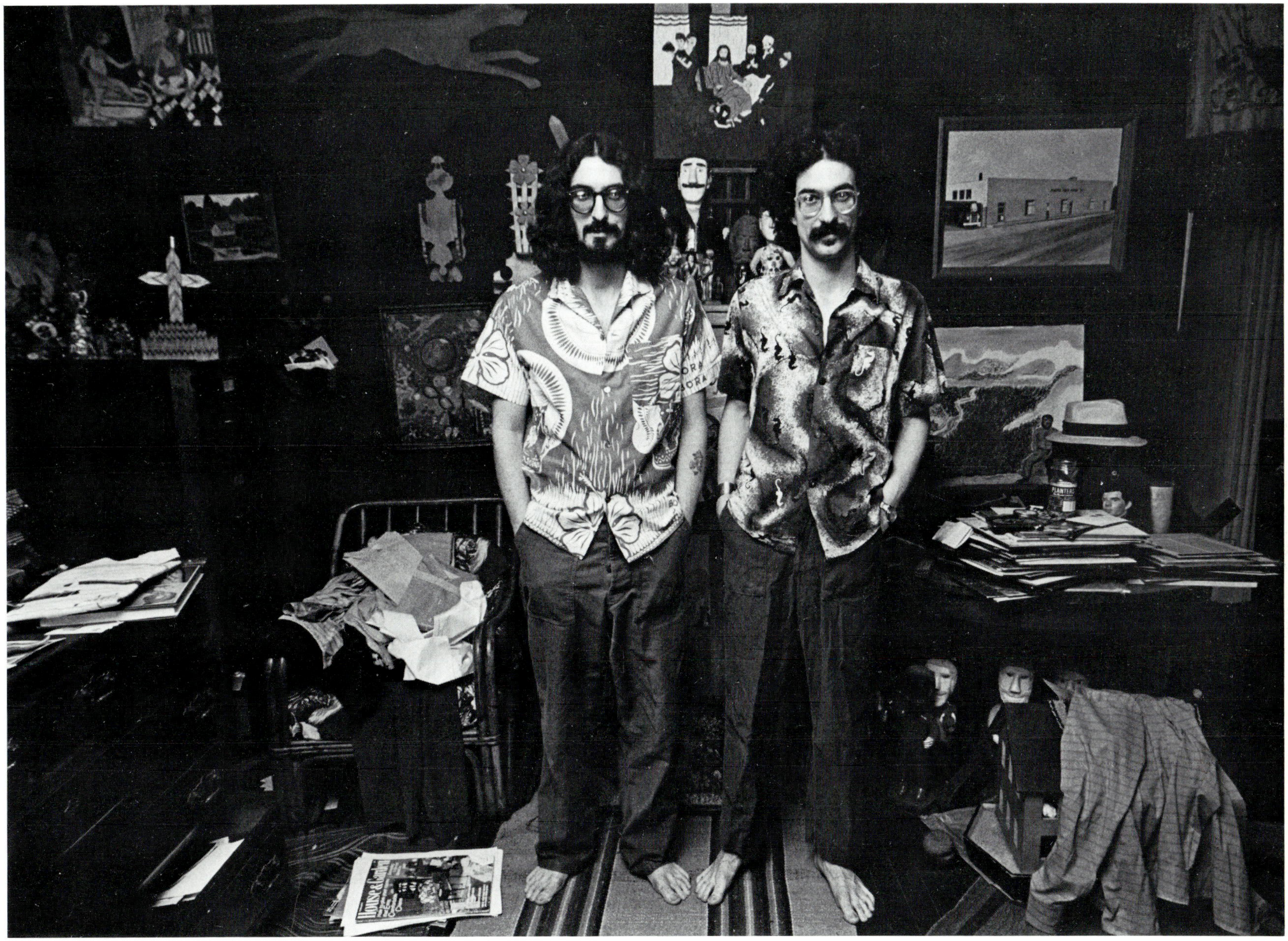

"As small children, we had a sense that we were closer than other children. We always had someone to play with. In school, we were loners because we were so close and we stayed together all the time—it was just the two of us. The first time we consciously dealt with our closeness was when we graduated from high school. While our schoolmates were crying and sad about leaving their friends, we just stood there and watched. We didn't feel close to anyone to be so upset. That's when we really felt that we missed something. We felt badly that we hadn't branched out to become close to other people. There was nobody that we were sorry to say good-bye to."

"To this day, I don't have a lot of friends and I still tend to cling to my twin. I don't make friends easily, particularly with women. I see women shopping or having fun together, and I think that I have my twin to do that with and if she's not available I stay at home. I don't feel comfortable with any other woman. I trust her and know her and know what to expect."

"Men seem curious to see if we are alike in all respects. My boyfriend had the audacity to ask me if I would ask my twin if we could have a little orgy together since he has this fantasy about being made love to by twins. He actually begged me. So I asked her and she said no. But he hasn't given up the idea yet. Maybe he's just got a problem. I told him we are built the same and our equipment is the same so *it*'s got to be the same, and so there's no need to have the orgy. But he mentions it every once in a while."

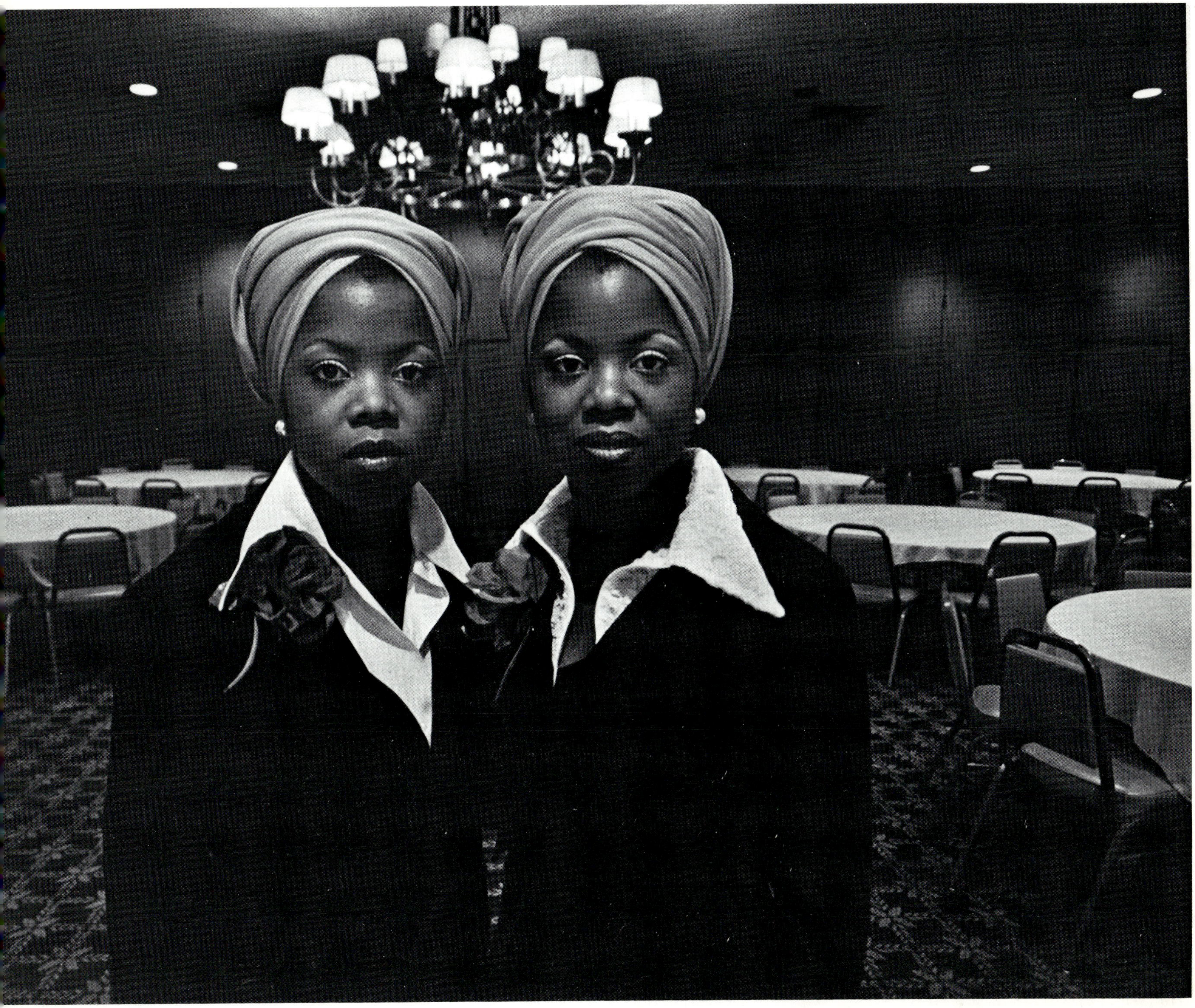

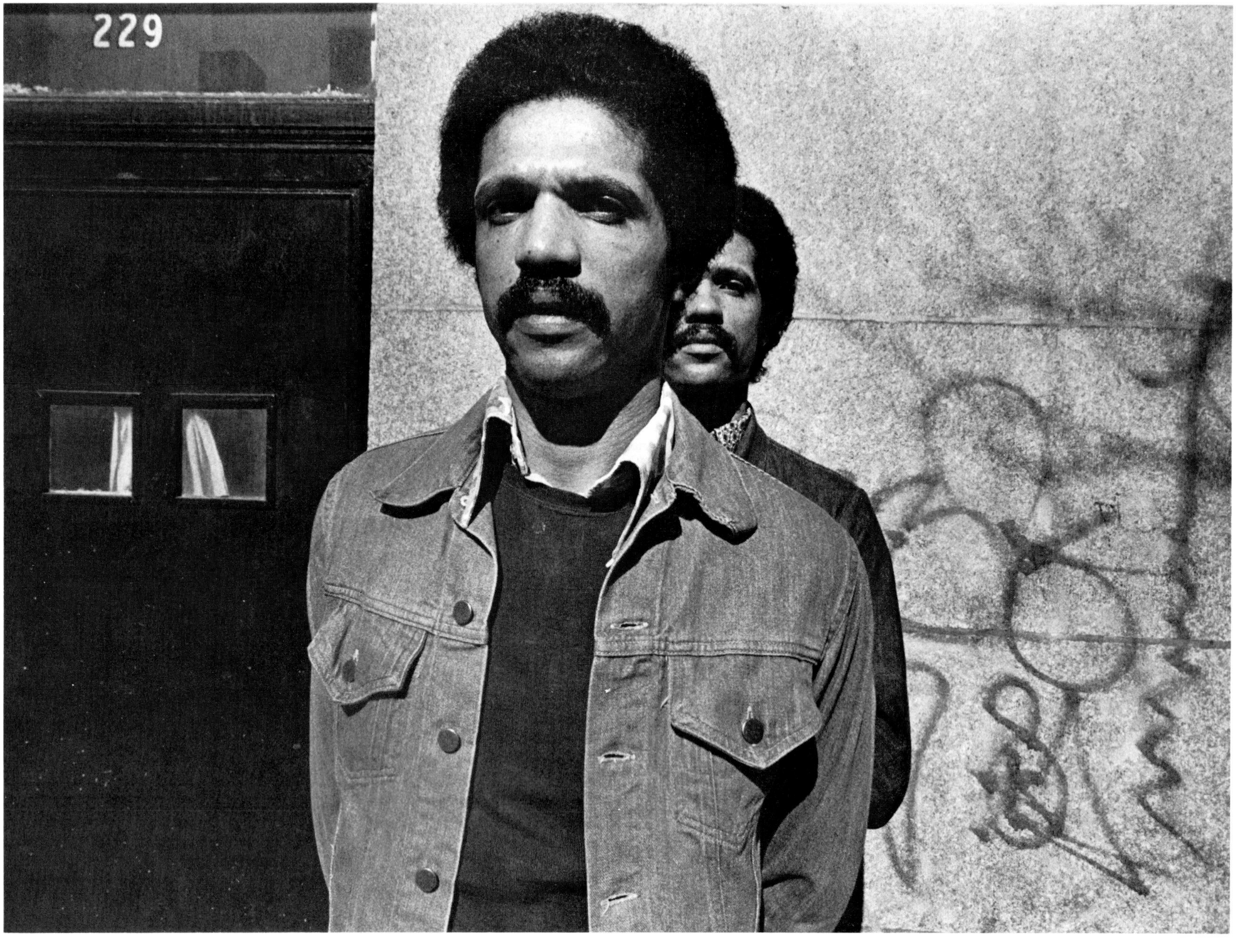
229

The Younger Twin:
"I recognize I am a copy. Ron is the original with an exact duplicate. Ron sets the pace. He has the jump on me. Therefore, he is in a superior position. But we have the capacity to be equal."

"We were separated for a long time. I lived out west; Ron was in Canada. When we both came to New York, we did not look very similar. If we had gone into a department store and bought identical suits, had our hair cut exactly the same, and then been put side by side, we would have appeared to be two individuals made up to look alike. But put us in a room together for a month or two and we would naturally start looking like each other." (*left*)

"I resent people's impressions of twins. It aggravates me when people say we are exactly alike. They make such generalizations—'Oh, you are so identical . . . the same eyes, voice, hair.' It hurts to hear this. I feel freakish when people stare at us, as if we were being dissected and automatically considered to be one person, like a record that's been duplicated."

"When we were 24, we both had long hair. My twin wanted to cut her hair—I didn't. She came home one day with short hair. I cried and cried and the next day I had my hair cut."

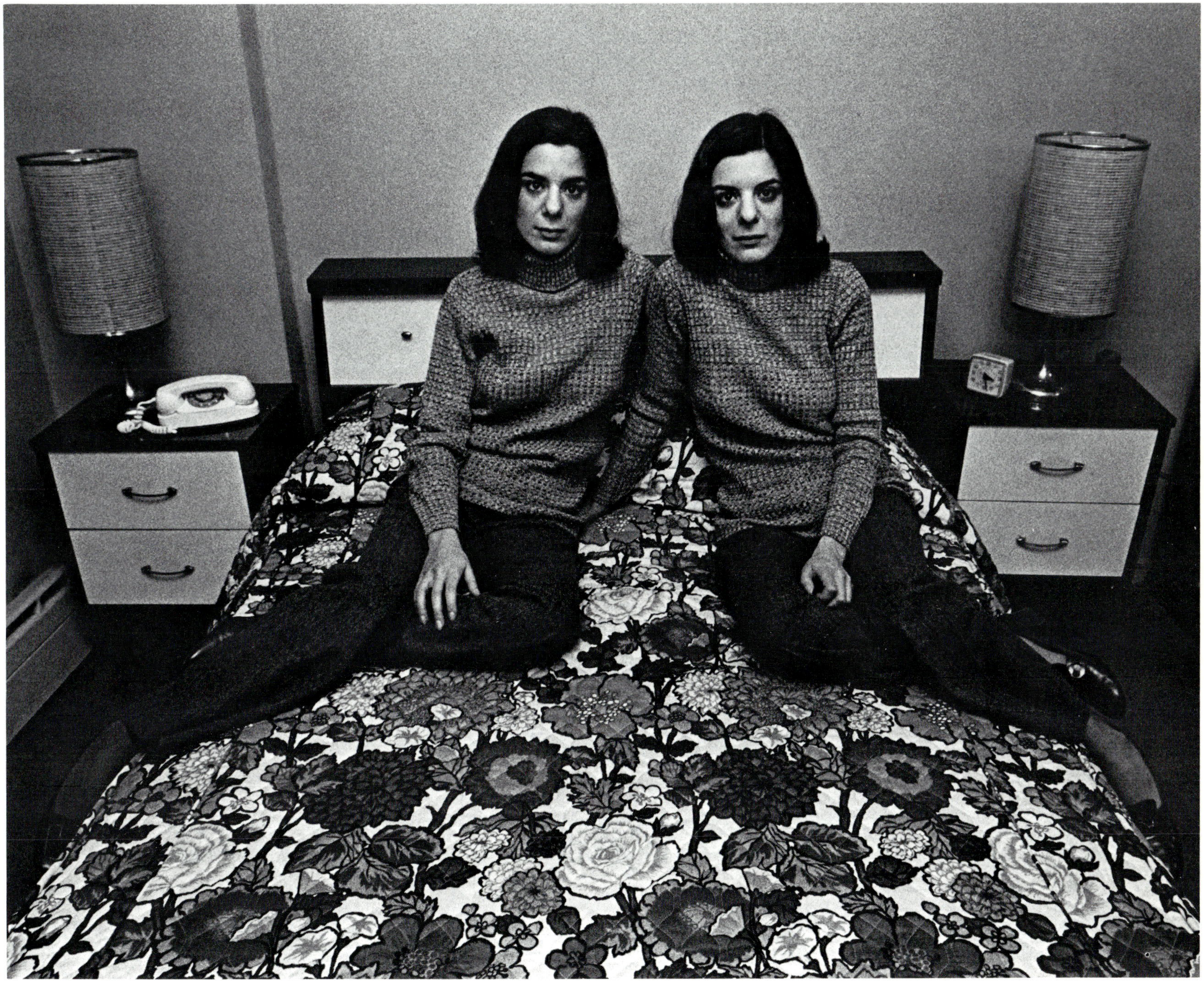

"Being twins retarded our ability to express ourselves because we seemed to possess telepathy. Even as teenagers, we had our own language; we'd speak in half sentences and made-up words. It was a shortcut and an easy way out. Now we spend lots of time developing our language skills."

"As twins, I always thought we were special. Then I realized the irony: being special implies a certain uniqueness but twins are two."

"I am totally attracted to the idea of twins. They are fascinating to me. It's a phenomenon and I'm very curious to see how other twins have gotten through it and how similar or dissimilar they are. I always compare the twins that I see to us and pick out the 'me' and 'my brother' in their relationship. It's one way I can tell them apart."

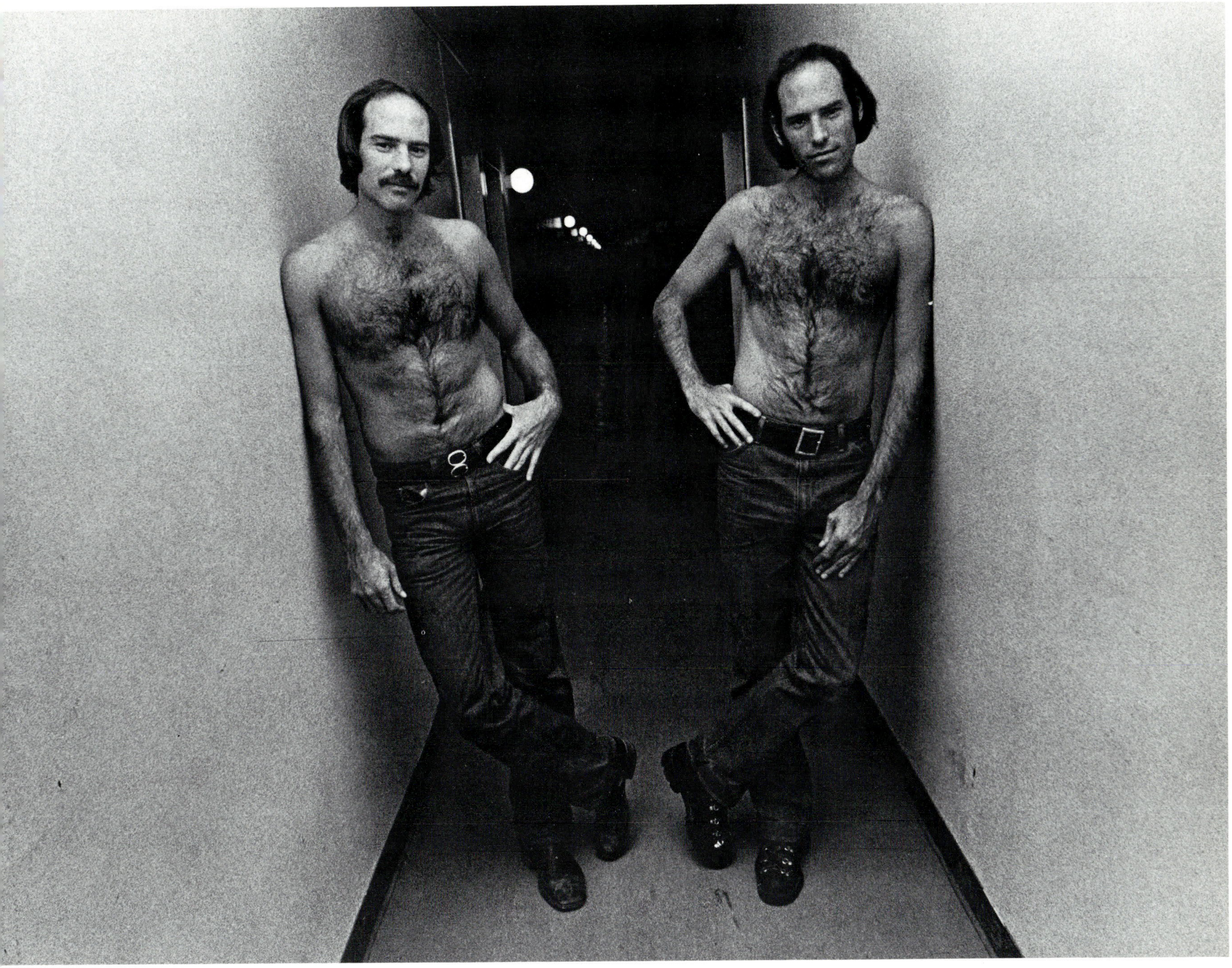

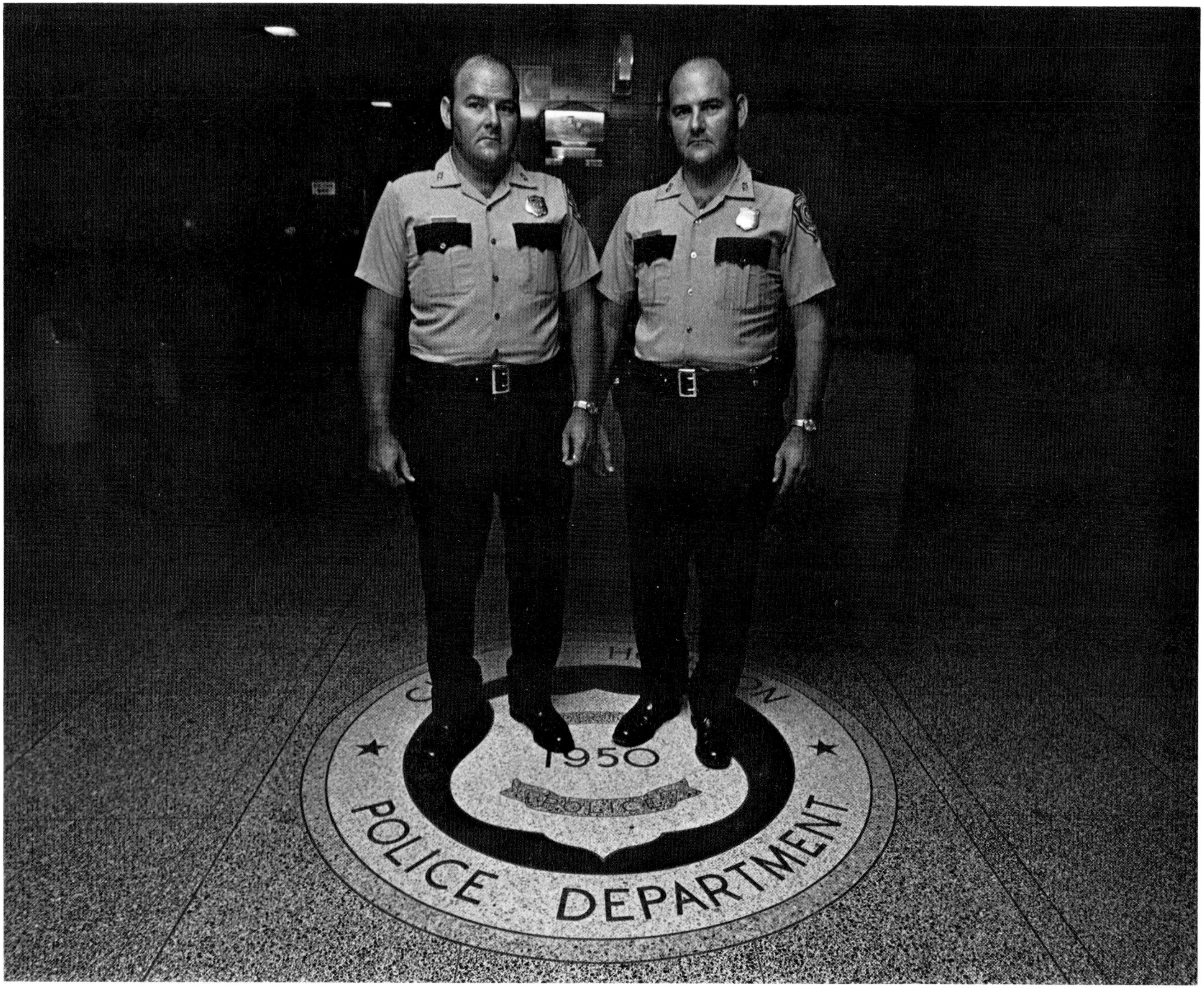
1950
POLICE DEPARTMENT

"We are both policemen; we work in the same squad and on the same shifts. I think the department put us together because they were afraid that if we worked separate shifts, we might substitute for each other without them realizing it. When on duty, I worry about my brother's safety, not mine. And I know he worries about me in the same way."

"When you are a twin, your body is a uniform. But when you put a uniform on top of that uniform, the twinness is accentuated even more."

Dick and Tom Van Arsdale are the only twins ever to play in the National Basketball Association. With 29,311 N.B.A. points scored between them during their twelve-year careers, they are the highest scoring family in basketball history and are only 2,108 points behind Wilt Chamberlain, the N.B.A.'s all-time top scorer.

In 1976 Tom expressed a desire to play on the same club as his brother. He was traded to the Phoenix Suns, thus reuniting the identical twins on the same team for the first time since they were students at Indiana University. A spokesman for the Phoenix team said they had sought Tom for eight years. At the end of the 1977 season, when they were thirty-four, both Van Arsdales retired to devote their energies to their real estate business in Phoenix.

Their twelve-year N.B.A. records are remarkably similar, the more remarkable considering the fact that they played on different teams (with different personnel, coaches, and playing styles) for eleven of the twelve years.

Twelve-Year Career Record

	Dick Van Arsdale	*Tom Van Arsdale*	*% Difference*
Games Played	921	929	0.9%
Field Goals Made	5,413	5,505	1.7%
Field Goals Attempted	11,661	12,763	8.6%
Field Goal Percentage	46.1%	43.1%	6.5%
Total Points	15,079	14,232	5.6%
Average Points Per Game	16.4	15.3	6.7%
Rebounds	3,807	3,948	3.6%

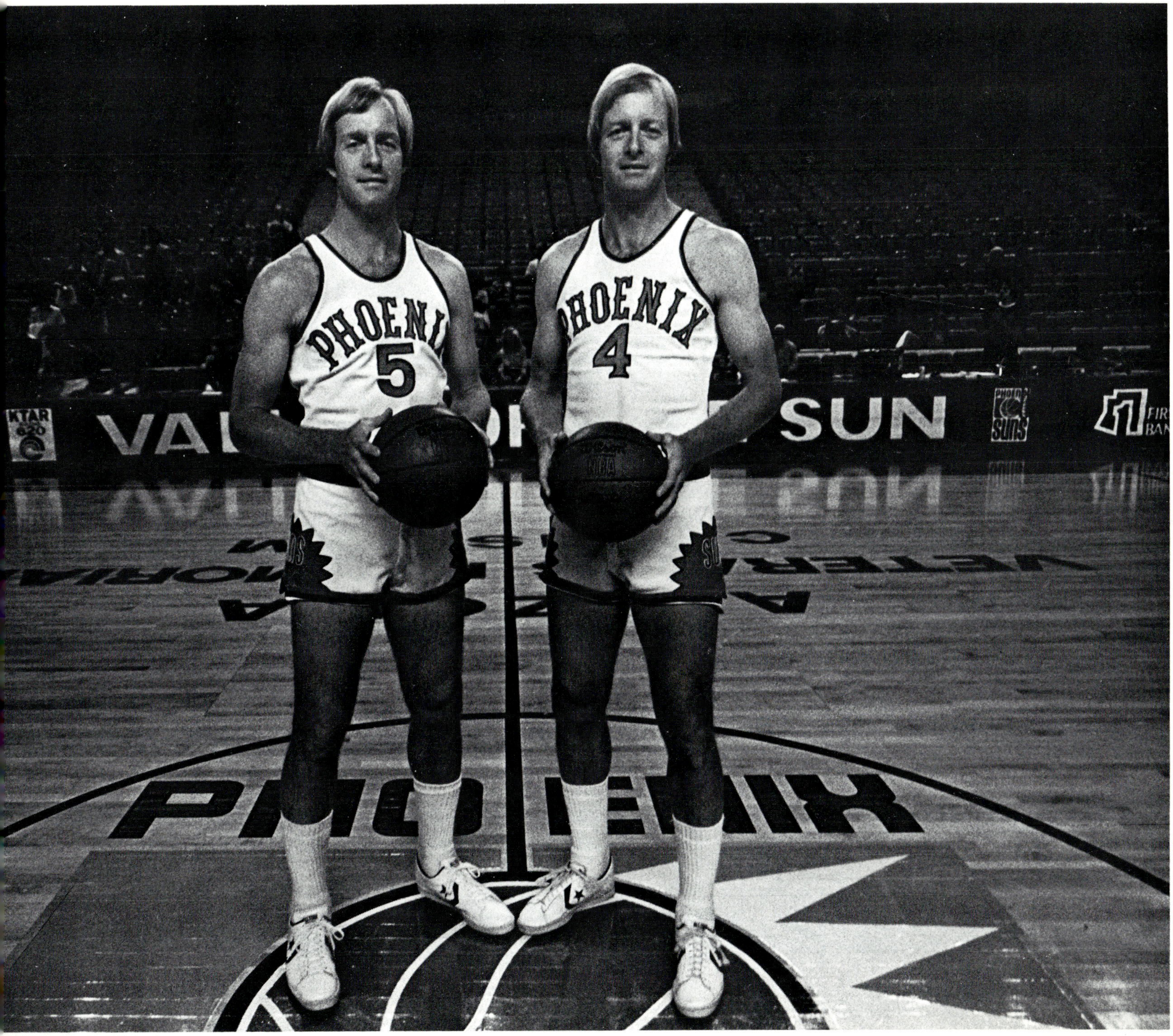
PHOENIX
5
PHOENIX
4
SUN
KTAR
620
PHO ENIX

"When my twin was very sick, I told her doctors that if she needed a transfusion, I did not want anyone else's blood in her but mine."

"I could never bear to lose my twin. I think I could accept losing my other brothers or sisters but not my twin. We have such a mental and psychological bond between us."

"Our children used to get us mixed up. As babies, they would hug me and ask, 'Are you my mommy?' They often did not know who to come to; if one got hurt, she would run to the closest twin for comfort, regardless of who the real mother was."

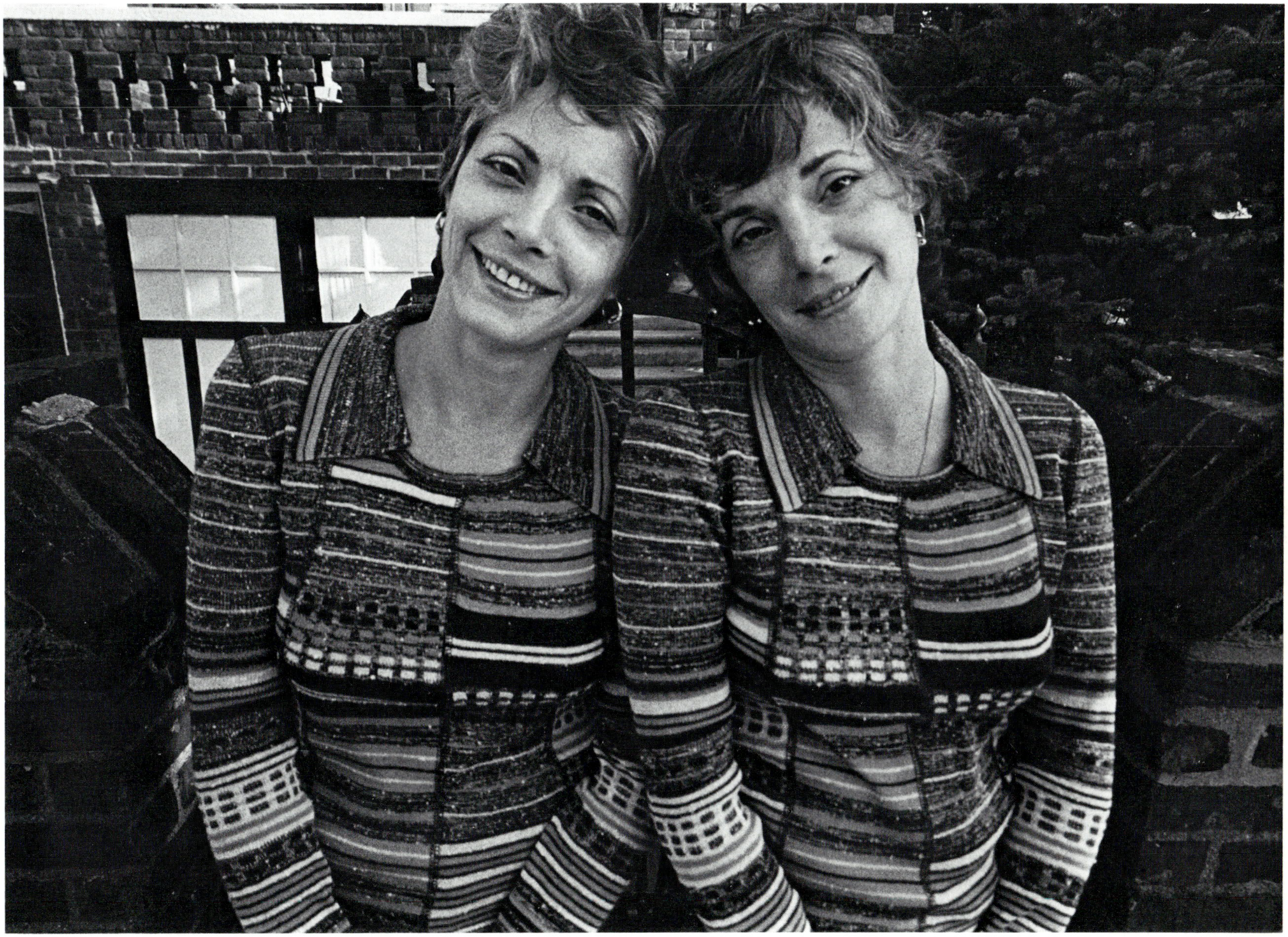

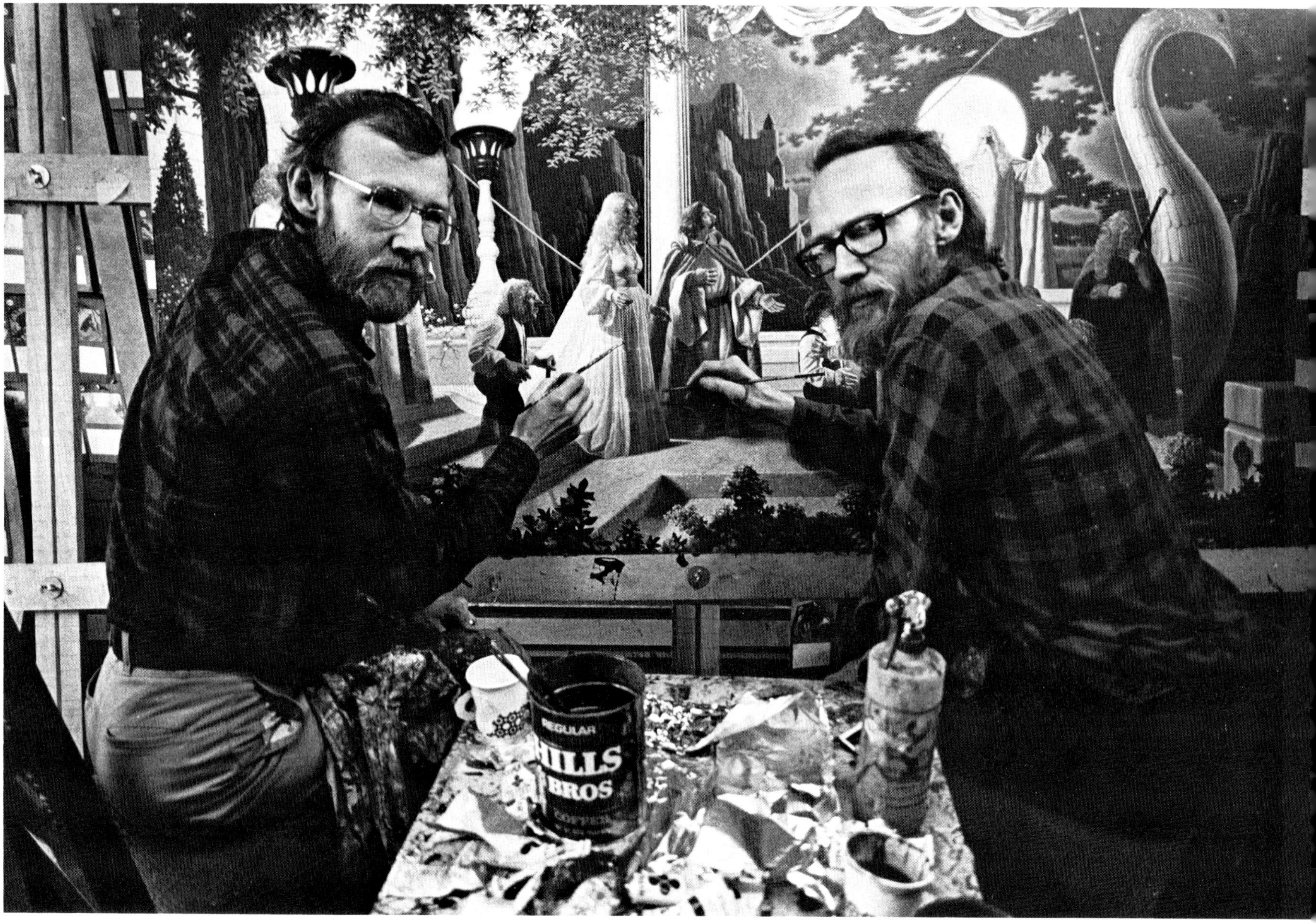
REGULAR
HILLS
BROS

Tim and Greg Hildebrandt are identical twins and fantasy painters, whose work includes the futuristic *Star Wars* poster and the illustrated calendars (1976–78) based on J. R. R. Tolkien's *Lord of the Rings* trilogy.

According to Greg, "We feed off each other and urge each other on. We are each other's inspiration and are always on the same wave-length. When we were kids and the other children were playing baseball or football, we were flipping out over the animation of the water in Disney's *Pinocchio*. We couldn't talk to our parents or schoolmates about it. But we discussed it with each other—we were our own best audience and still are."

They refute the notion that a work of art must be created by one individual, citing the history of large mural paintings, the collaboration of Rubens and his staff of assistants, and even the studio of Walt Disney, who had up to six hundred artists animating his films. As Tim says, "Our paintings are a total collaboration and our talent is exactly alike. Regardless of whether Greg or I paint a figure, it looks the same. We do it all together, from initial ideas to sketches to the finished work. We haven't painted anything individually for years and now would never think of doing that. We sign only our last name to our paintings. It's a joint ownership; it's our painting, not Greg's or mine."

And Greg adds, "We start the painting together, literally working on it side by side. Then Tim might take it home and work on it for a few days. Eventually, he'll bring it to my studio where I'll probably work on it or we'll paint together. I might go to sleep while Tim paints and then he'll sleep while I continue the painting. We never wake up to see something we don't like. When I awake, I see that more is done. It's like magic—I'm sleeping yet the painting progresses. A single artist cannot experience that. When Tim paints, it's as if I'm painting; I feel as though I'm doing it without really having to do the labor or the thinking."

"Neither of us wanted to be dentists. In fact, we both hate it. Ever since I can remember, our father wanted us to be dentists. He had a friend who was a successful dentist and thought it would be good for us too. He felt a certain duty to prepare us to be self-supporting. He was compulsive and unreasonable and never encouraged us to make choices. So dentistry was drummed into our heads. In those years, kids knuckled under. But our temperaments are just not suited for dentistry. Anyone with a romantic spirit wouldn't like it; there's no stimulation and little gratification. We are basically daydreamers.

"We work together at a dental clinic once a week. We were raised to be together. It was easier for our parents to deal with us as a package rather than one of us running here, the other running there. Emotionally we are still very close, so to see my twin hurting and unhappy disturbs me very much. That's why we'd never have a full-time practice together. It would be destructive to our relationship to always work together and see each other so unhappy and disappointed."

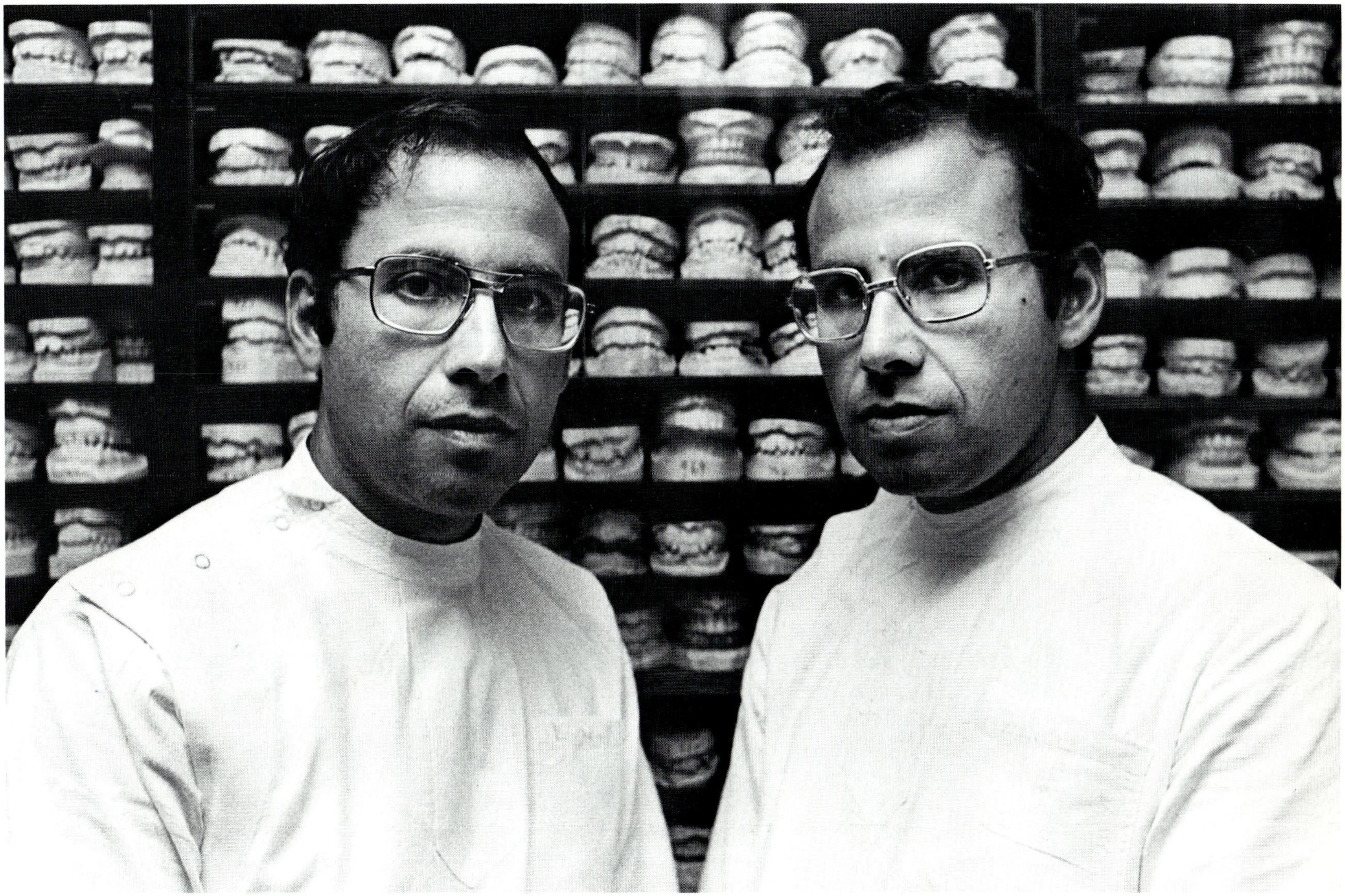

L̲avona:

"We knew each other three years before we started dating. After about two months of dating, they proposed to us. And we were married six months later. They proposed in unison. Amazingly, we felt they would propose the evening they actually did.

Al:

"We left their house that night and I said to Art, 'Should we give them rings for Christmas?' We decided to ask them the next night. So the next day we bought rings and went to their house and almost immediately said, 'We've got something to ask you.' They nudged each other and started grinning even before we said anything else. We got on our knees together, asked them to marry us, and they accepted in unison."

Lavelda:

"When I started dating Art, I knew he'd be the one. We had a feeling for each other. I didn't feel that way about his brother. If I had initially paired off with Al, I don't think there ever would have been a marriage. I feel something towards my husband that I can't feel towards his brother. I like them both but there is a much deeper and special feeling for my husband. I enjoy having him near me. I want him with me. Even when I reach out and touch him I have deep feelings. Just because we are identical-looking, we are not interchangeable and don't have desires for the other's spouse."

Lavona:

"When a teacher in high school tried to put us in different classes, I stood up to her and said 'Hands off, someday we're going to marry twins and have twins and there is nothing in your power to ever do anything about it. It's within us; we have to do it.' When she came to our wedding, she reminded us of this incident—we had forgotten completely about it."

From Twincerely Yours *by the Rowe–Richmond Twins, Volume 5, Number 1, page 15 (1977):*

"Among the guests at the Rowe–Richmond wedding were thirty sets of twins. Twins served as bride matrons, bridesmaids, flower girls, and junior bridesmaids. There were twin dolls on the cake, twins serving the punch, twin hostesses, twin organists, and twin entertainers, along with twin cakes, of course."

LAVONA:

"As soon as you walk through the front door of our house, you see a large picture of me and my husband on the front wall. Right next to it is a big picture of my sister and her husband posed exactly like us. But unless you knew that twin married couples lived in the house, you'd think someone was very vain to have two identical pictures hanging on the wall. We've tried to make the house appear as a one-family house because we feel we are one family. Our bedroom furniture is similar but not identical since we are using furniture we owned before our marriage. But when we buy new bedroom furniture, it will probably be identical."

Ella and Lila Wigren of Arlington Heights, Illinois were one of the original sets of Toni Twins in the early 1950s. Nationally known, they participated in the advertising campaign for about five years, their pictures appearing in magazines, on billboards, and in department store displays. The heading, "Which Twin has the Toni?" challenged the reader to guess which twin had her hair coiffured in an expensive beauty parlor and which had set her hair at home with a two-dollar Toni kit. The ad found its way into American folk humor and became a classic example of successful advertising (it was revived and updated for television in 1977).

More recently the Wigren twins have been in the news as a result of their participation in an Indiana University study utilizing twins to determine the effects of heredity versus environment on certain medical variables. Statistically they are one of the most nearly identical sets of twins yet discovered in this study, having

—exactly 153 ridge counts on their fingerprints
—same toe prints
—identical eyeglass prescriptions
—same blood pressure, heart rate, and cholesterol levels
—similar tooth problems

"One researcher told us we are so identical that we could be one person." Even now, their identities are confused by their husbands, children, and friends. "I've been kissed in public many times by my twin's husband. My husband thinks it's funny.

"We were absolutely identical at birth. As a matter of fact, it's possible that Ella is really me and vice versa. No one knows if the right person has the correct christened name. The doctor was going to mark one of us (perhaps with a tattoo) to tell us apart. Then he found a birthmark on my hairline. To identify us, Mother always had to check for that birthmark."

Toni CREME SHAMPOO
...For Soft Water Shampooing
even in the hardest water
WHICH TWIN HAS THE
Toni

Braun Hobby
Braun Hobby
ELMO
ELMO
ENSIGN
Nikon
BINOCULARS
Braun 2000

"When we were children, our playmates thought that we should not get full shares of anything that we might be dividing up. Because there were two of us, we should each get one-half as much. The funny thing is that adults constantly do the same thing to us."

"We dressed exactly alike until we were thirty-nine years old—until we got out of the Navy. For twenty years, we were stationed together with the exact same jobs. We got our promotions at the same time, no sooner or no later than the other one. Our desks were always back to back. Boy, did people ever get us mixed up.

"We now buy clothes that are exactly alike but usually don't wear them at the same time. People would bother and hassle us too much. If I wear my green sports coat today, and he wears his next week, it seems like I'm wearing the coat again. It gets awfully tiresome."

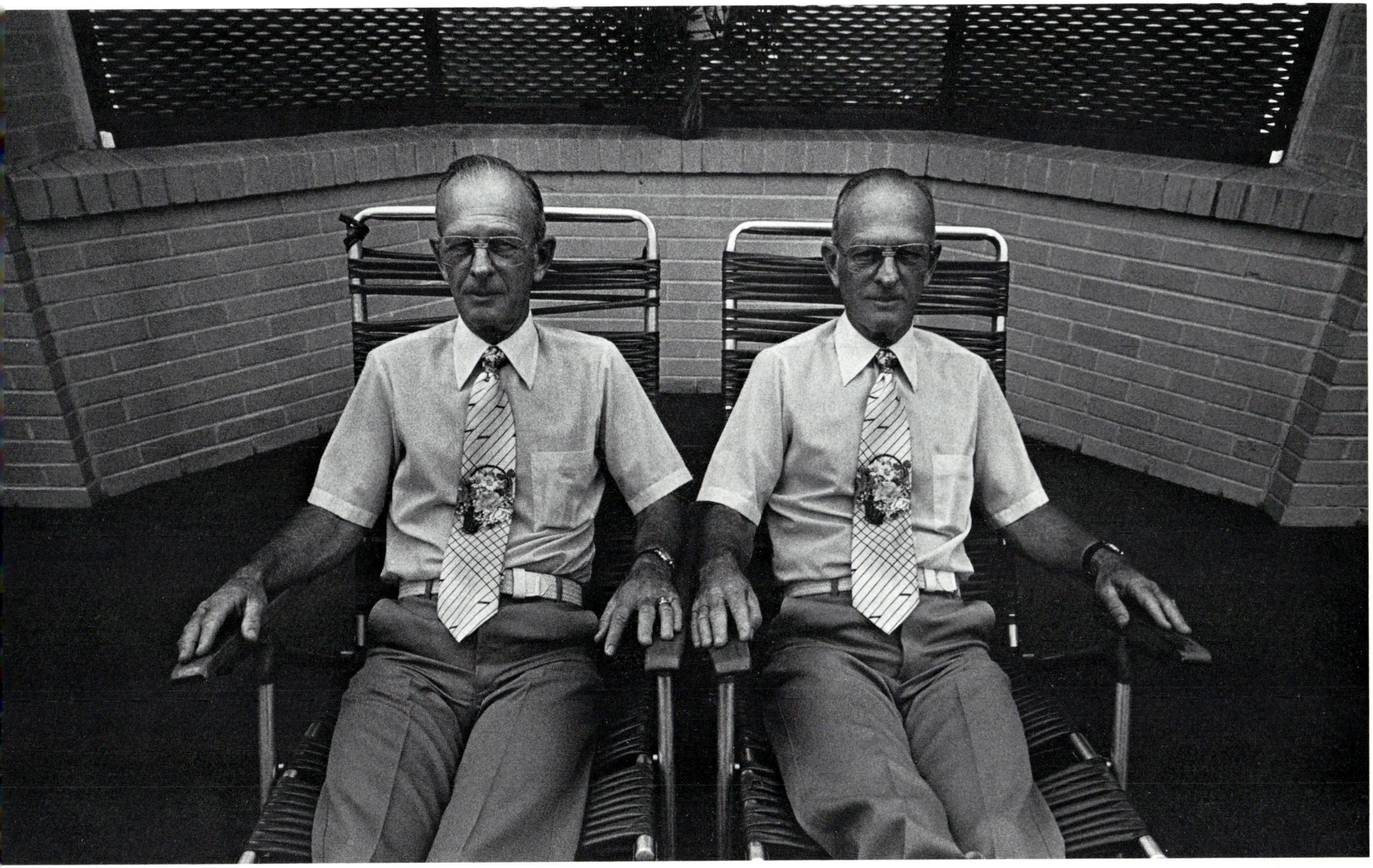

"In 1923, when we were five years old, Siamese twins came to the local vaudeville theatre in Brooklyn and were presented as an act. The Brooklyn *Daily Eagle* advertised that any twins could enter the theater free. We were taken by a friend of the family. I remember that the red velvet curtains opened and we saw these twins dressed in red velvet costumes trimmed with gold braid. They were attached at the hips; they were at an angle to each other and couldn't sit straight forward. I didn't know what I was seeing. It never occurred to me that such a joining could be possible. No one had ever explained it to us.

"Between them was a red velvet tablecloth with a gold fringe. Whatever tissue or membrane bound them was covered with this red velvet cloth. . . . They were young women with breasts and they spoke with a foreign accent of some kind. I don't remember what the act was about. I just remember two pretty ladies on the stage. After the act, we were taken backstage. I don't know why. When we were taken into their dressing rooms, it hit me. I realized that these two lovely looking ladies couldn't get up and walk. They seemed to be in an invalid situation and I realized that something was very, very wrong. A feeling of horror came over me because, by that time, we were very aware that we, too, were twins, and that one of us could run down the street and the other run up the block. But here were two people bound to each other who couldn't run. I didn't know how they were tied to each other, but I knew it was something more than the red velvet material and that something was horribly wrong. I wondered what was under the red velvet because, obviously, we didn't have anything like that.

"We thought the Siamese twins might have been under a spell of some kind, or had a curse put on them. At home we acted it all out. I remember getting safety pins from the sewing box next to grandma's bed and then joining together our knee-length dresses with the pins. We walked around and finally tore the dresses. It was terribly confining. At that time, life was much simpler than now without television and radio—we acted out many, many things which was very healthy. I think we acted it out enough to get the trauma out of our systems.

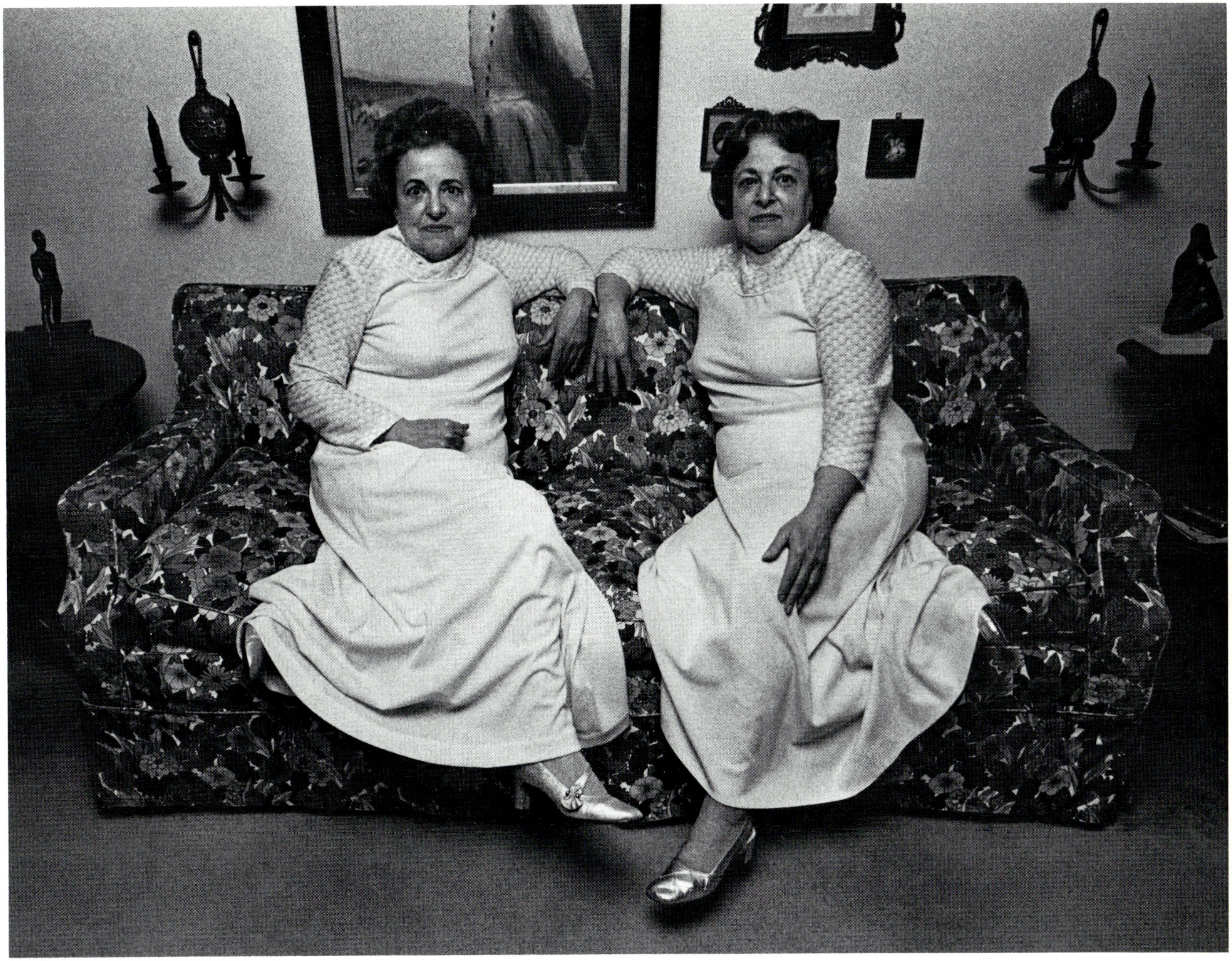

"In 1944 I was at home in Illinois and my twin was in the Army in the Pacific. I knew he was missing in action the day after it happened. This was well before we received official notification. It just hit me. I became upset and angry with the whole world. I'd just go out and take walks for miles by myself. I didn't talk to anyone. My relatives thought I was cracking up. Two months later, I suddenly felt better and I knew my brother was safe. Weeks later, we received word that he was O.K."

"I can't see myself growing old until I see it in my twin. When I realize that my twin is graying, I realize that I am graying and my own self-image has to come to grips with growing old. Having a twin makes ageing very graphic."

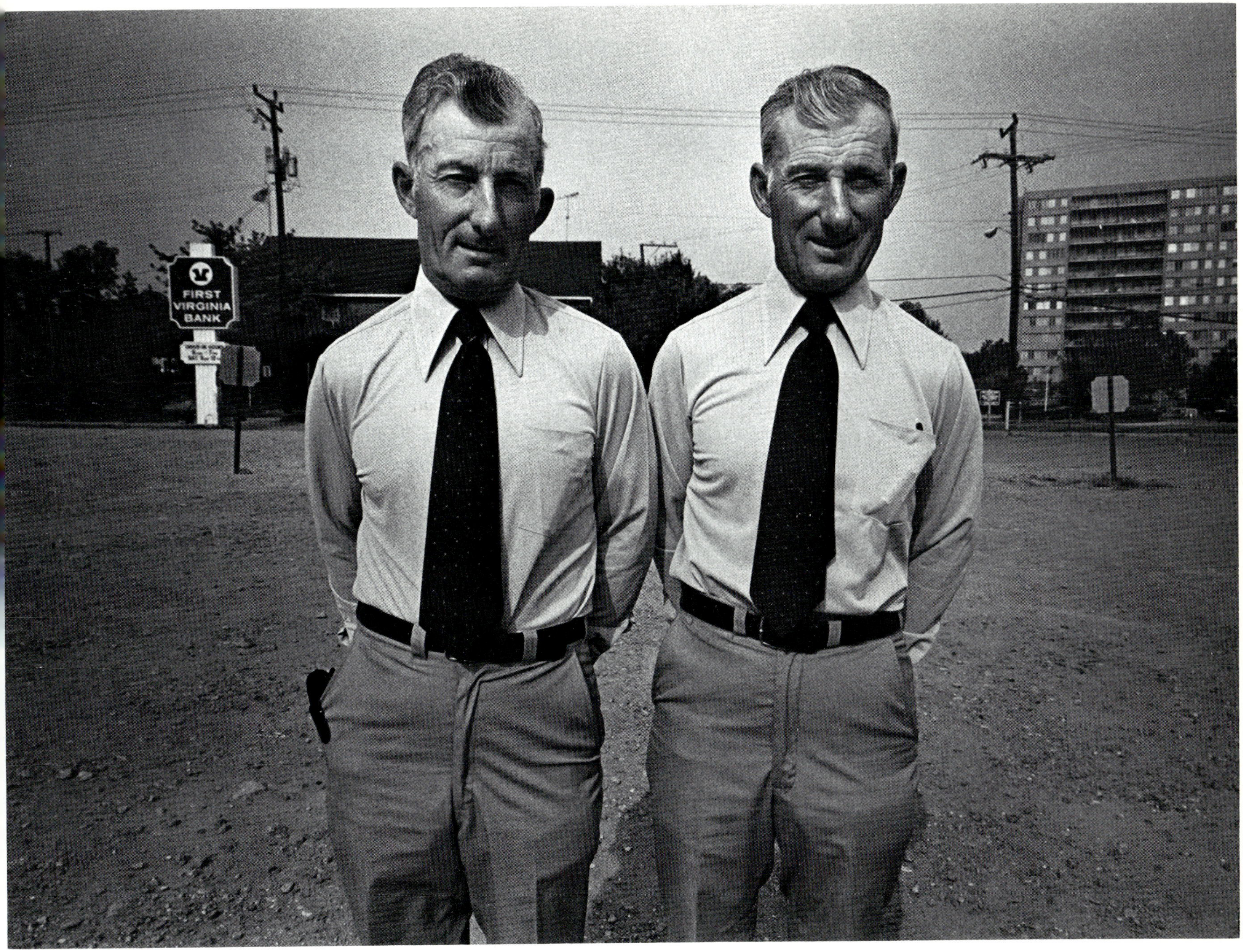
FIRST
VIRGINIA
BANK

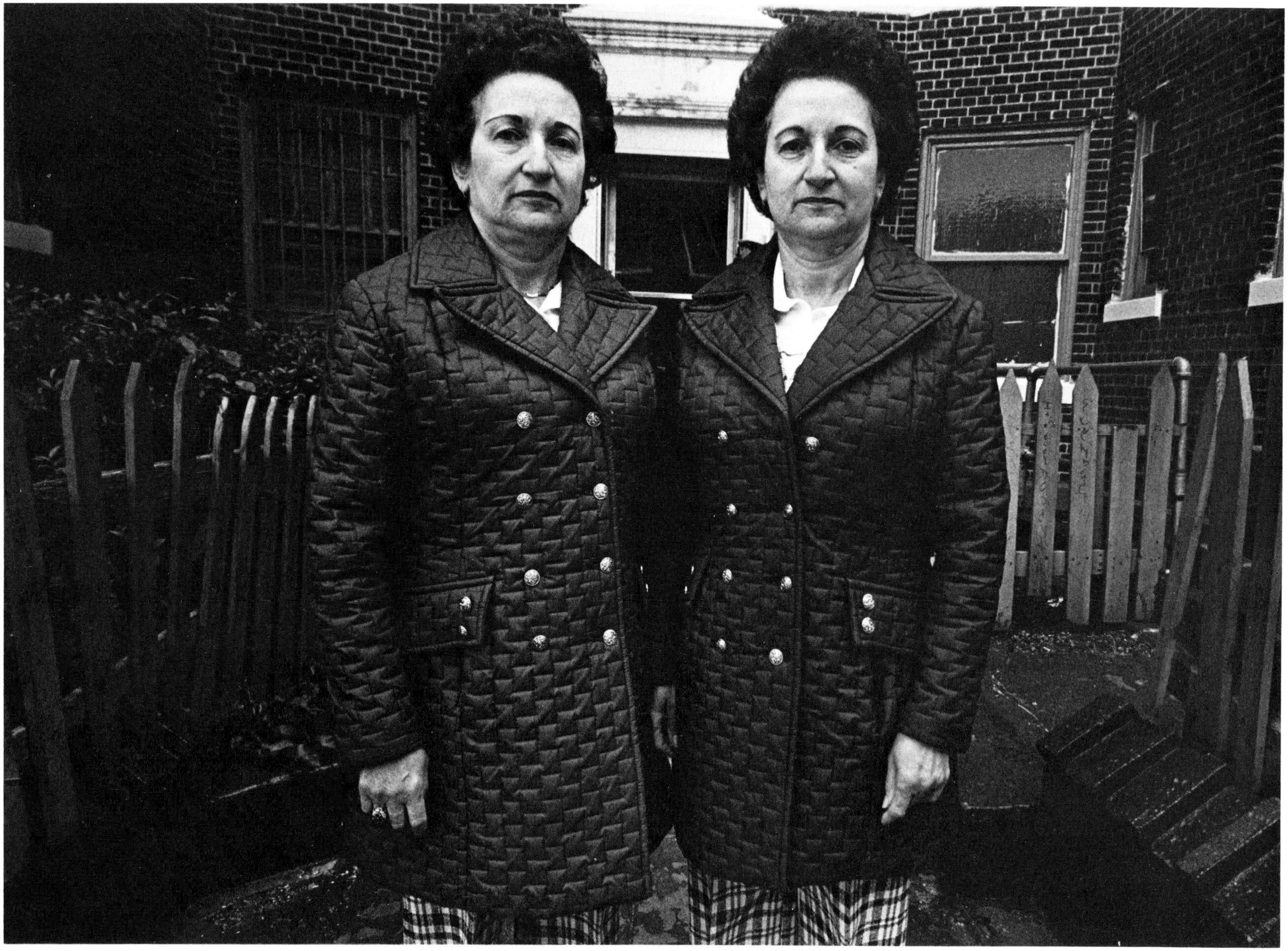

"We still call each other every morning before we go to work and then when we come home. You tell a psychiatrist this and he'll say it's bad. The telephone bills are enormous. That's who we're working for, the telephone company. We talk about our day, our careers, what we'll wear. In the morning, we wish each other a good day. This started when our mother died in 1961. Mother was an early riser and would call each one of us each morning between 8 and 8:30. When Mother died, I said to my twin, 'That call in the morning to begin the day is full of life and full of joy. Let's start it, Mother would like it.' We've been doing it ever since. When I'm on vacation, I write long and voluminous letters to my twin. The letters are like talking to myself. She saves and returns them to me so I don't have to keep a diary."

"Teachers could never distinguish us. Even if we dressed differently, it didn't help them. Then one day, in junior high school, a teacher gave me a wide white rubber wristband to wear. When I raised my hand, the teacher knew who was responding. This caught on and I had to wear the wristband throughout my high school years. I still have the damn thing."

"When we were in our early twenties, we were offered a year-long contract to appear in advertisements for a hair-coloring product. The contract stipulated that one twin had to shed fifteen pounds while the other twin had to remain at her current weight. Even though the financial rewards were great, we refused because we didn't want to be that different for so long a time."

"Our husbands feel we collaborate with and influence each other. They don't have as much control over us as they would like, probably because we are twins and are very close. They have been called by each other's name because of us."

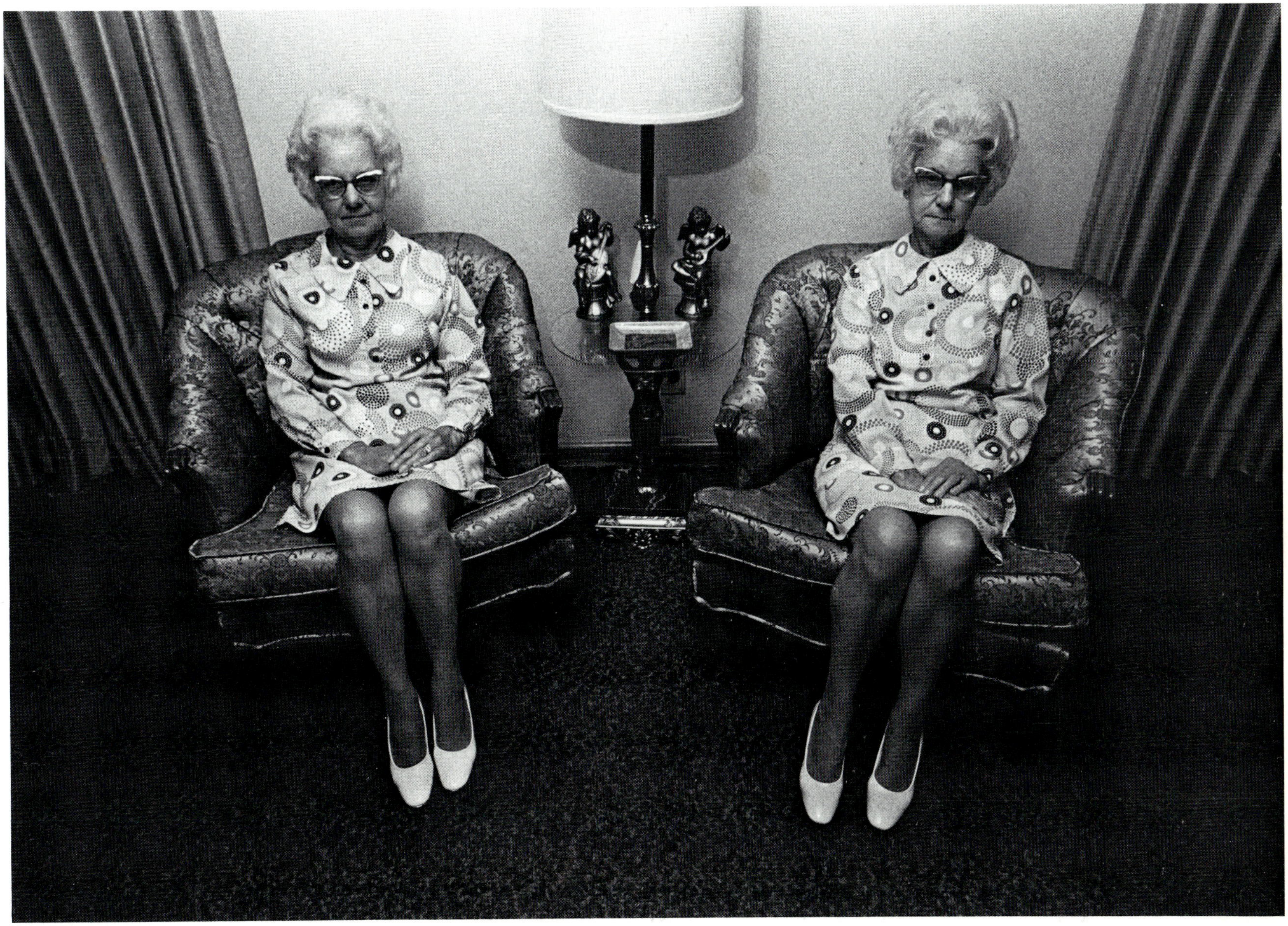

"We are individuals even though we dress alike. It's too bad that parents today don't dress their twins alike. These parents are listening to too many psychologists. Because of this, twins are missing a lot of fun. I know if I had had twins, I would have dressed them alike."

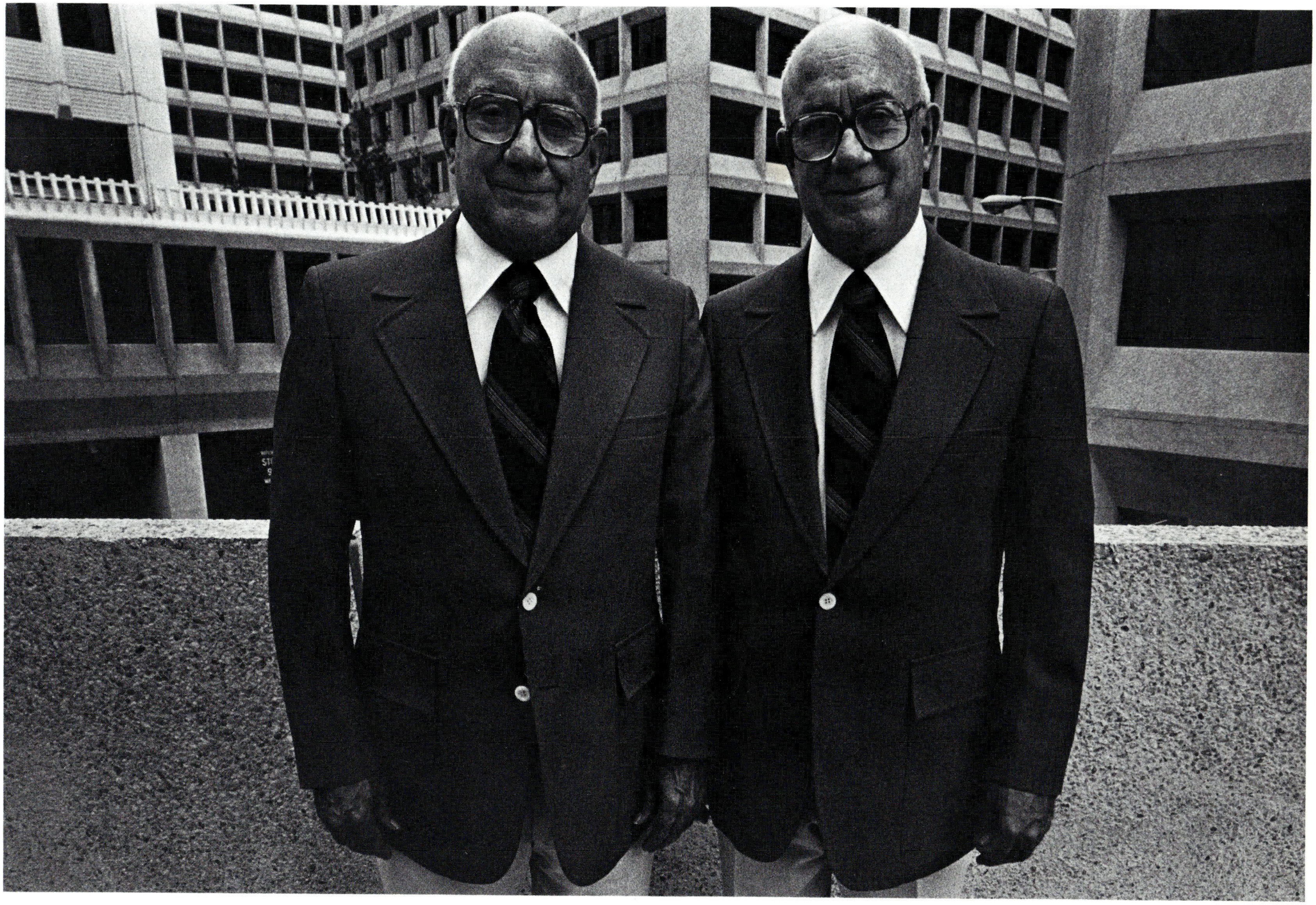

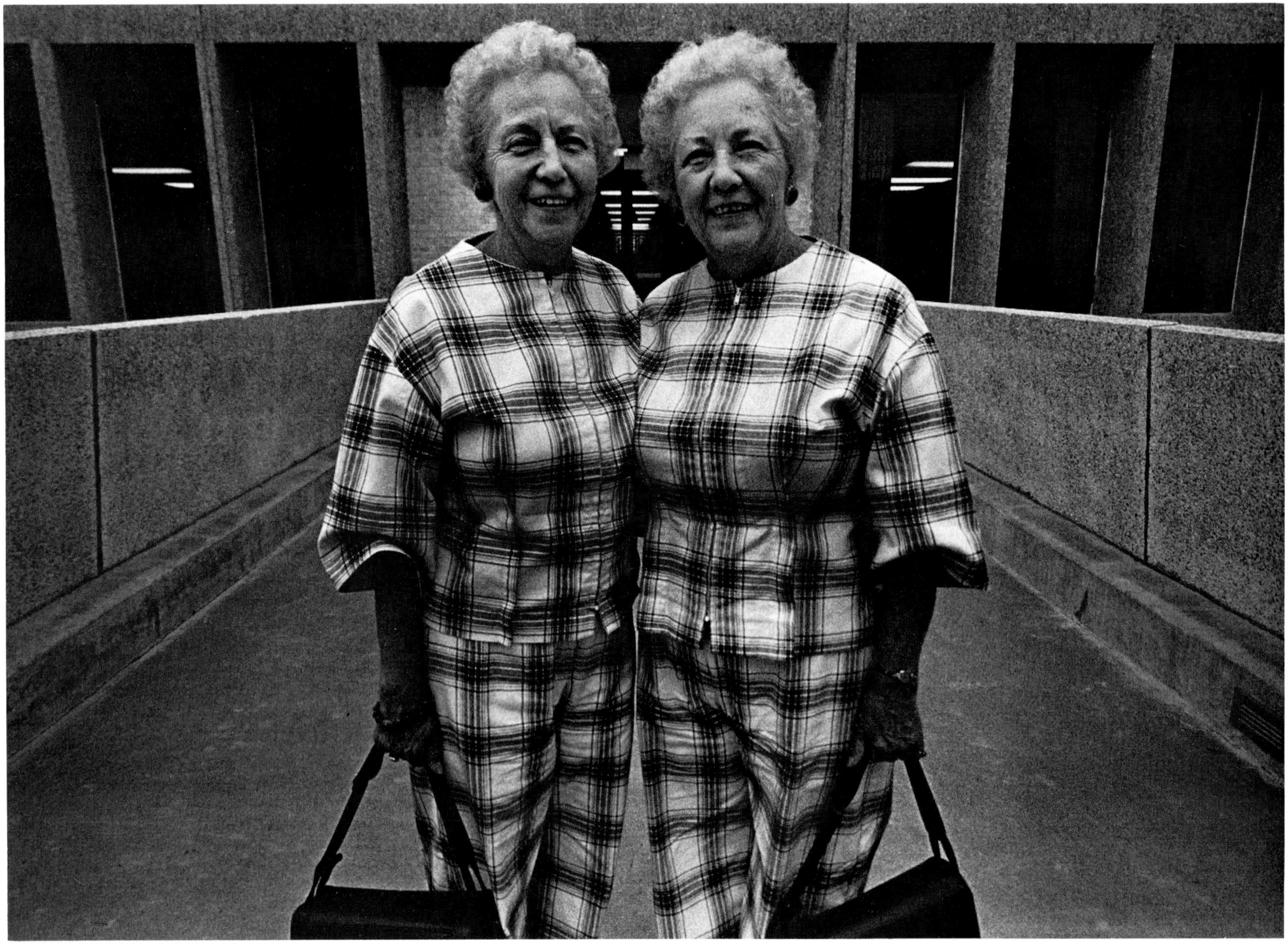

"We wouldn't think of ever wearing clothes that weren't identical—it would never enter our minds. We are asked frequently: 'It's so unusual to see people your age dressing alike and looking so much alike. Why do you do it?' That question never comes from twins because they understand, they know the joy of being a twin."

"I cannot imagine what it would feel like and be like not having my twin. I don't want to imagine it. When the time comes, then I'll think about it. We've never talked about this with each other."

"People tend to shy away from us because we are different. They feel we are unsettling to look at and to be with."

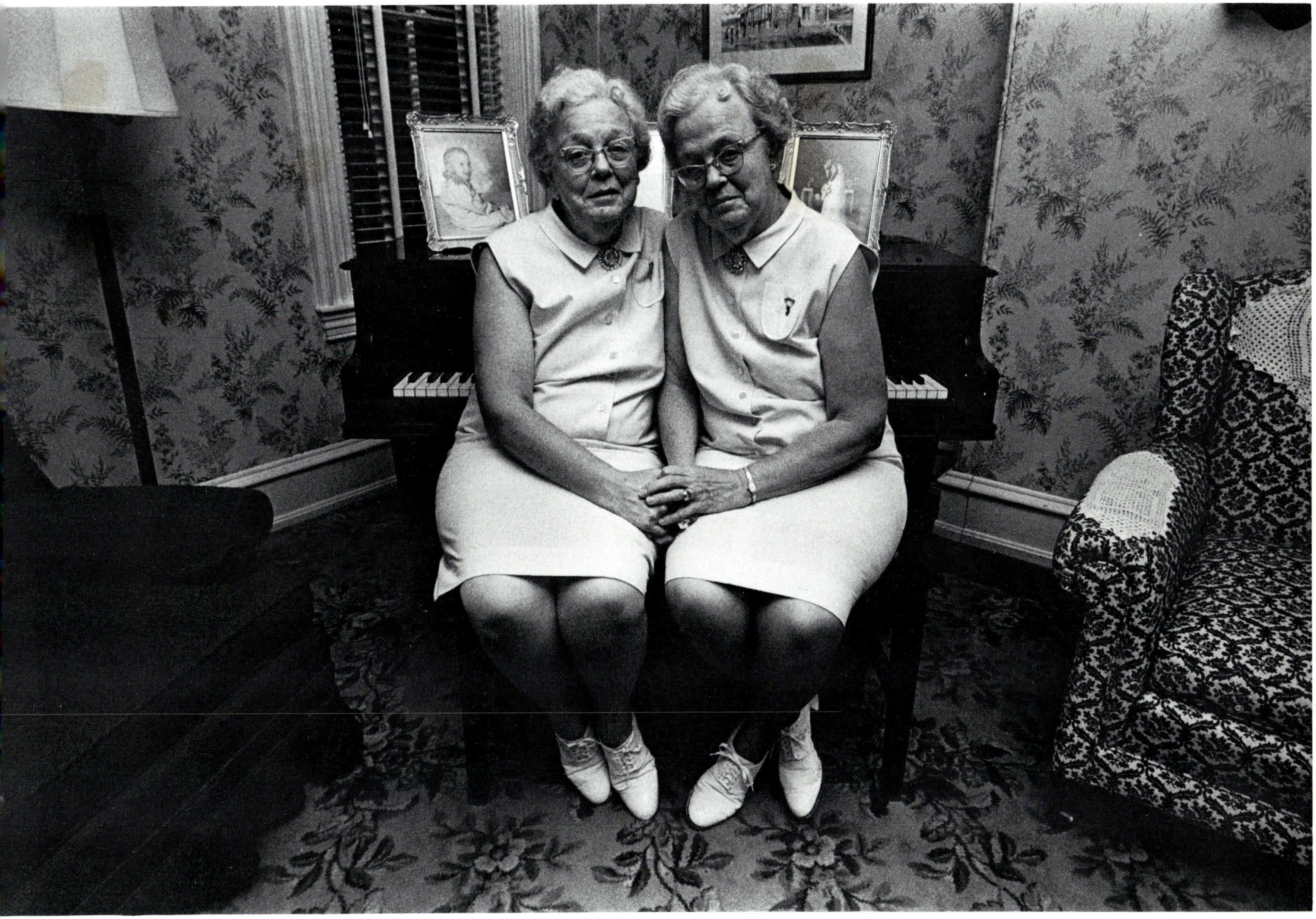

John and Raymond are seventy-one years old and Irish. They sleep in the same bed in a single room on New York's Upper West Side. Neither has ever married, though Raymond hints that he did live with a woman once. He has a girlfriend now, and walks six miles a day, to and from Twenty-third Street, to see her. Asked whether they enjoy being twins, they shrugged, with John beginning, "It's like a Jewish friend we have; he was asked if he liked being Jewish." Raymond interrupted and finished, "Our friend answered, 'Who knows—ask my mother. I didn't have anything to do with it,'" and they broke out laughing together.

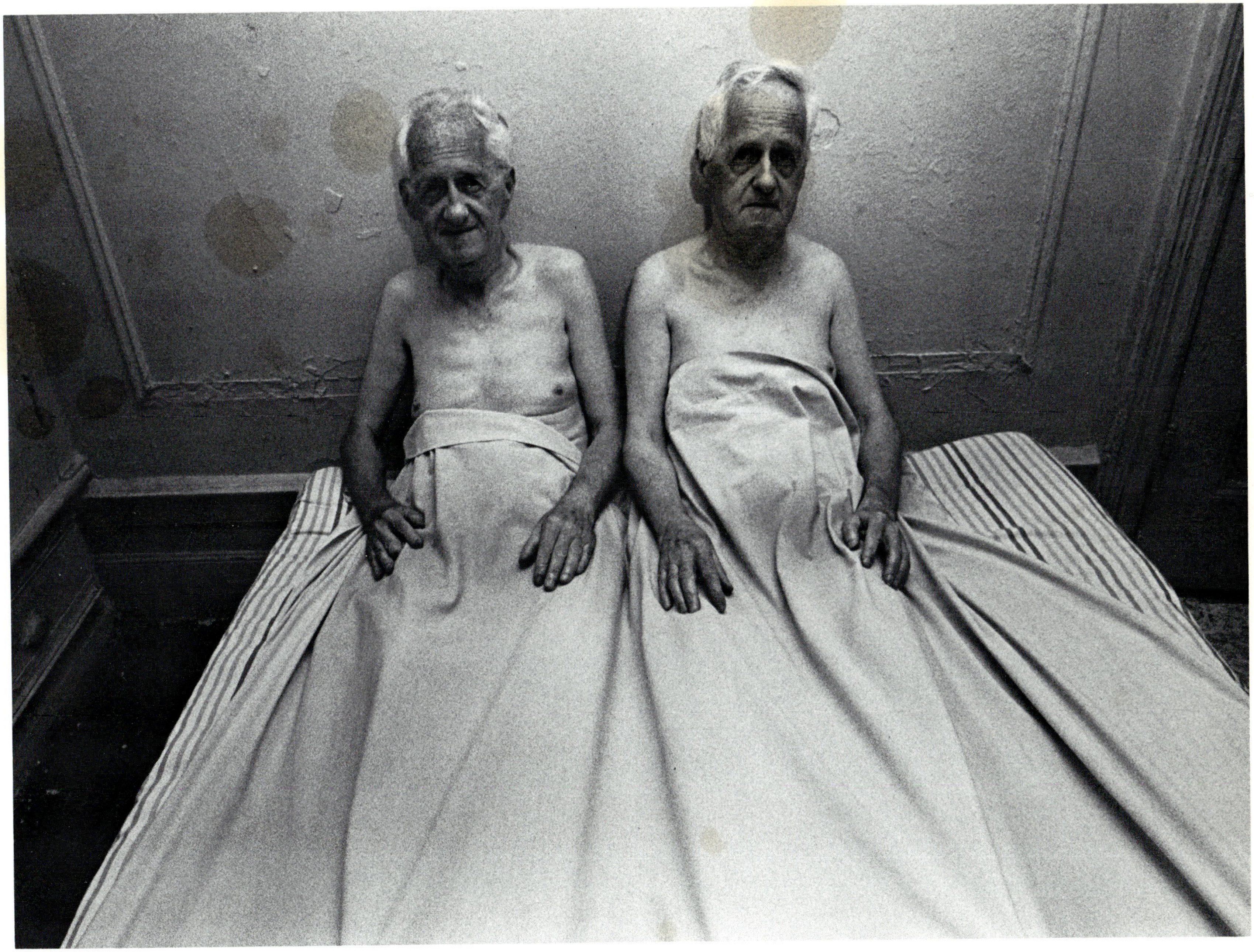

Bibliography

Direct quotations in the text not attributed to published sources are drawn from interviews conducted by Ted Wolner.

Direct quotations accompanying the photographs are drawn from interviews conducted by Harvey Stein.

In preparing the text, the following books and articles were particularly useful:

Arlow, Jacob A. "Fantasy Systems in Twins," *Psychoanalytic Quarterly*, XXIX (1960), 175–199. The section dealing with Jonathan McCullogh is a reconstruction of this article.

Brain, Robert. *Friends and Lovers*. New York: Basic Books, Inc., 1976. Chapter 6, "Friends as Twins," was helpful.

Burlingham, Dorothy. *Twins: A Study of Three Pairs of Identical Twins*. London: Imago Publishing Co., Ltd., 1952. By far the best analysis of the psychology of twin children.

Fiedler, Leslie. *Freaks*. New York: Simon and Schuster, 1978. The text draws on Chapters 1, 8, and 13.

Freud, Sigmund. "The Family Romance of Neurotics." In Rank, Otto, "The Myth of the Birth of the Hero," *Nervous and Mental Disease Monographs,* 1914.

———. "The Uncanny," *Collected Papers,* Vol. IV: *Papers on Metapsychology.* International Psychoanalytic Library, edited by Ernest Jones, M.D., No. 10. New York: Basic Books, 1954.

Hartland, E. Sidney. "Twins." *Encyclopedia of Religion and Ethics,* edited by James Hastings, XII, 491–500. The most comprehensive overview of the anthropology of twins. The research on twins in aboriginal societies was largely done in the years from 1900 to 1950. It is impossible to check on which societies still retain intact the ritual practices and beliefs reported in the text.

Hugo, Victor. *Les Jumeaux.* Paris: Hachette, 1927. This story was later developed and expanded by Alexandre Dumas as "The Man in the Iron Mask."

Kallman, Franz J. "Twin and Sibship Study of Overt Male Homosexuality," *American Journal of Human Genetics,* IV (1952), 136–146.

———. *Heredity in Health and Mental Disorder.* New York: Norton, 1953.

Lacombe, Lucien. "The Problem of the Identical Twin," *International Journal of Psychoanalysis,* XL (1953), 6–12.

Larousse Encyclopedia of Mythology, entries under individual names of twin gods.

Leonard, Marjorie. "Problems in Identification and Ego Development in Twins," *Psychoanalytic Study of the Child,* XVI (1961), 300–320.

Loeb, Edwin M. "The Twin Cult in the Old and the New World," *Miscellanea Paul Rivet.* Mexico, 1958.

Oatman, Jack G. "Folie à Deux," *American Journal of Psychiatry,* XLV (1942), 642–645.

Rank, Otto. "The Double as Immortal Self." *Beyond Psychology.* New York: Dover Publications, 1958.

Scheinfeld, Amram. *Twins and Supertwins.* Baltimore: Penguin Books, 1973.

Stevenson, Isobel. "Twins as Magicians and Healing Gods: Twin Myths," *Ciba Symposia,* II (1941), 695–701.

About the Authors

HARVEY STEIN, a professional photographer, has exhibited his work in numerous one-man and group shows here and abroad. His photographs have appeared in many books and periodicals, including *Time, Life,* the *New York Times, Camera, Harper's,* and *Popular Photography*. He currently teaches at the International Center of Photography in New York City.

TED WOLNER, himself a twin, is a writer whose articles have appeared in the *Village Voice* and *New York* and *Harper's* magazines. He holds a doctorate in American Studies and is presently at work on a cultural and intellectual history of city development in nineteenth-century America.

/BF 723 T9S74 1978 00001

**Library and Learning
Resources Center
Bergen Community College**
400 Paramus Road
Paramus, N.J. 07652-1595

Return Postage Guaranteed